# Acknov

A book may be written alone, but it is given its wings by others. I'd like to acknowledge all those who contributed to the launch of this book:

Shawn, Joe, Jeremy, Justin, Dustin, Tree, Corey, Mike, JP, Cit, Lyna, Ava, Elise, Jill, Richard, Alexis, R. Moores, theCrookedHouse, and my sister Debbie.

I would also like to thank all the incredible and gracious people in the horror fiction community on Instagram, for their encouragement, never-ending support, and love.

*Ceremony of Ashes*

# CEREMONY OF ASHES

*A Novella*

Jayson Robert Ducharme

*Ceremony of Ashes*

# October 31ˢᵗ

# Waxing Crescent

The sun went down and it was time for all the ghouls and ghosts to come out.

Not all of them were nasty creatures of the night. There were superheroes, cartoon princesses, and even a few futuristic knights straight out of a spacy fantasy movie. They dashed through the pale night, going from house to house, emerging in the stoop lights waiting for treats with bags in hand. Strobe lights flashed while cardboard monsters danced in fake cemeteries made of plastic headstones. It was a cold night, but not too cold. Another Halloween in Leinster Village, like dozens before.

Going up Bradley Avenue was a young woman with a little girl dressed as Snow White, wearing a yellow dress and a red bow tied in her dark brown hair. The girl trotted up to the front porch of a house where a werewolf stood wearing a plaid coat and jeans. The wolfman gestured with fierce, curled fingers, dropped a few candies into the girl's bag, and then snarled at her. The girl ran back to her mother on the sidewalk, gigging and shrieking, and wrapped her arms around her leg.

"I hope you won't give my daughter any nightmares tonight, Ted!" the mother called.

The man in the werewolf mask waved. "She's a big girl now, Clarissa! I don't think a big hairy dog will scare her!"

"Yeah!" the girl said defiantly. She let go of her mother and planted her knuckles on her hips. "I haven't been scared once this whole night!"

Clarissa ran her fingers through her daughter's hair. "I'll see you around, Ted!"

"Happy Halloween! Stay safe, Julia!"

A couple of kids—a superhero and a bloody zombie—came running across the lawn, and Ted the werewolf got back into character. Grinning, Clarissa rested her hand against her daughter's back. "C'mon, hun. We still got another hour."

At six years old, this was Julia's first Halloween. As a parent, it was Clarissa's first as well. She wanted to take her daughter out the year before but (and she would never admit to it) Julia was always afraid. With all the macabre decorations, the abstract lights, and the monsters running around, Julia was always too scared to go out. This year, though, Julia proclaimed that she wanted to do it no matter what. Of course, she *was* scared—Clarissa could tell by the way her body tensed and her breathing grew rapid as they left the driveway—but with each house they went to, the girl's confidence grew. Halfway through the night, Julia was rushing from house to house, and Clarissa had to jog to keep up.

"Julia!" Clarissa called. "Slow down!"

The little girl came running back from a house, the plastic wrappers of the candies in her bag rattling as she went. "I have so much! Can we do this tomorrow?"

"I'm afraid it's just this evening, sweetheart."

"I don't want it to be over."

"I don't want it to be either. I'm having a lot of fun."

Clarissa noticed that the streets were starting to clear and some of the houses were shutting off their lights. "Things are winding down now, Julia. Let's go home and count the bounty. Maybe we can lie down and watch a movie."

"Okay. But I don't want you stealing all my stuff."

"You want to keep all the ones with nuts in them?"

"Oh yuck!"

Clarissa laughed and took Julia's hand. "Your first Halloween accomplished! Did you have fun?"

Julia grinned, her baby teeth beaming proudly. "Yeah. I wanna do it again next year."

They walked through the dark neighborhood. The sound of laughing children and chattering teenagers gave way to night crickets chirping and the occasional faraway dog bark. They crossed the intersection of Clydesdale and Tenney Street and went down Tenney until their only company was the street, the sidewalk, and the woods. Ahead, a single streetlight glowed. It acted as the lone beacon between one neighborhood and the next.

"Sure is dark," Clarissa said. "Stay close to me, kiddo."

"Look!" Julia pointed.

There was someone walking towards them—a shadow in the distance. Leather heels clomped against the pavement.

"Who is that?"

"Just someone in a costume, Julia. Stay close to me."

It was a woman. As she approached the streetlight, Clarissa could make out her features better. A veil masked her face like a gloomy curtain, and she wore a black dress with long leather gloves that went up to the elbows. Black from head to toe—she seemed more like a mirage in the dark than a person.

The woman stopped and waved as they met at the streetlight. "Happy Halloween, mademoiselle."

"Happy Halloween," Clarissa said, walking faster.

"If I may have a moment of your time?"

"We really have to get back home."

"Scary costume!" Julia exclaimed. She stopped, enamored by the woman.

"Thank you for the compliment, ma chérie. I must say, you look beautiful yourself." The veiled woman pinched her dress and gave the little girl a polite curtsey. "Is this your first Halloween?"

"Yep!"

"And what are you dressed as?"

"Snow White."

"Come on, Julia." Clarissa tugged on her daughter's arm. "I'm sorry, miss. We really must be going."

"You seem alarmed," the woman pressed. "I'm sorry. I live just down the street. I've been passing out candy and performing magic tricks for all the trick-or-treaters."

"Magic tricks?" Julia's face lit up.

"Correct." The woman laced her fingers together. "My name is Angelique de Lapointe. I've lived here in Leinster Village for some time."

Clarissa stepped forward. "I've lived in the village my whole life. I've never heard of anyone named Angelique or DaPont."

"It is *de Lapointe*," the woman tactfully corrected.

Clarissa squinted at the woman's veil. Vaguely, she could see the shape of a face and a single milky eye, but nothing else. The way the woman talked was peculiar—a mishmash of accents. French, but not quite.

"Well," Clarissa said, again tugging on her daughter's arm, "it's been a pleasure, Ms. Lapointe, but we have to go now."

"Mom! What about the magic trick?"

"Yes, maman," Angelique piped in. "One magic trick, and I will let you go."

An irritated sigh left Clarissa. "Fine."

The woman clapped. "Magnifique! Okay, Snow White, listen closely." She knelt and pulled a black handkerchief from one of her long gloves and handed it to Julia. "Take this and inspect it."

Julia pinched the handkerchief by the corners and looked it over back to front.

"Now, stuff it into my hands." Angelique cupped her hands into a ball and left a small gap between her palms. The little girl stuffed the handkerchief into the gap and stepped away. Angelique brought her hands close to her veil, whispered something, and then put them up over her head. Once separated, a raven fluttered from her palms, embracing newfound freedom.

"Wow!" Julia exclaimed, pointing.

Clarissa, amazed, followed the raven with her eyes as it settled on a branch above them. It let out a loud squawk. She couldn't believe what she was seeing.

Angelique bowed. Julia jumped up and down in excitement. The hostility Clarissa felt towards this stranger eased, and she smiled and applauded the showwoman.

"That was stunning!" Clarissa said. "How did you do it?"

"Ah-ah!" Angelique held a finger up. "I never tell my secrets. Otherwise, there is no magic."

The bird lifted a wing and began pecking at its ribs. Above the bird, the moon hung within the night sky in her lunar infancy, resembling a yellow toenail clipping rather than a celestial rock.

"The moon sure is beautiful tonight, isn't she?" Angelique said. "She is in waxing crescent now. The beginning of the lunar phase. The cycle is supposed to finish in twenty-nine days, but I think it will end sooner than that. The moon and I—we are sisters."

Clarissa raised an eyebrow. "You said you live here in Leinster?"

"Yes, just off this street."

"I seriously don't recognize you."

"You will soon. Here, I'll give your Snow White a treat and let you be on your way."

The woman dug her hand into a leather purse slung from the bend of her arm.

"Thank you, lady!" Julia said, holding out her little treat bag.

Clarissa's grip on her daughter's arm grew tighter. "How long have you lived here exactly, Angelique?"

"Oh, shortly before I met my fiancé. 1947, I believe."

Clarissa blinked. "How old are you?"

"As of this past August, I am one hundred and six, Mademoiselle Holloway."

"What? What are you—"

Angelique flung her hand from the purse and black soot blinded Clarissa and Julia. It burned their eyes and sent ash down their throats. They coughed and wiped their faces, swatting at the lingering smoke in the air. Once their lungs cleared and their vision slowly returned, they heard a methodical clicking sound.

The shape of Angelique materialized before them. She held a metronome, the needle clicking rhythmically left to right.

"Shhh," she whispered. "Listen to me very carefully."

Clarissa and Julia did not flee, yell or resist. Both followed the metronome needle with their eyes. Consciousness slipped away from their pupils, leaving empty windows in their faces.

"Tres bien. I want you to pay very close attention, Clarissa and Julia Holloway." With one hand holding the clicking metronome, Angelique raised the other and gestured for the two to follow her. "Come with me. Stay close. You understand?"

The mother and daughter followed the woman out of the streetlight and into the woods. The raven on the branch squawked, and then swooped off, following them.

The night deepened, and Leinster went to sleep. In the woods, the veiled woman stood beneath an opening in the trees, gazing up at the moon. In one hand she held a ratty doll made of twigs and old cloth. The other hand dripped with warm blood. Red drops fell from her fingertips onto the brown and orange leaves at her feet. Quietly, she whispered something, and then held the doll up to the moon and smeared its face with blood.

"There will be nothing but ashes," she said.

It began.

# November 1ˢᵗ
# First Quarter

Leinster Village is slow to wake.

Daylight crept over the river, casting a dark blue hue against the old colonial houses with chipping wallpaper and rickety front porches. A lone SUV patrolled the dark neighborhoods with its exhaust coughing smoke in the chilly morning air. It stopped now and again so that Craig Campbell—Leinster's aging and overweight paperman—could waddle out and jog from lawn to lawn to pitch newspapers onto people's stoops.

Wrappers and discarded candies littered the sidewalks from the previous evening's festivities. The bell of the Leinster Presbyterian Church—an ancient, wooden thing with faded stain glass windows—rang a Sunday morning chime from its steeple. The spire of the steeple pressed against the sky like an obelisk.

Few souls were awake at seven o' clock that morning. Among that few was Constable Colquitt Kaysen and Delores Hamilton.

"Every year I have to deal with these little shits!" Delores cried, shaking a veiny fist in the air. She was wearing a nightgown and her hair was filled with curlers. "People don't know how to discipline their kids proper nowadays. If I did something like this as a child, my ass would be red for weeks."

Constable Kaysen stood, her eyes half open, listening to the old woman. She wore a scarf with a heavy police coat and gloves, yet the only part of her that felt warm was the hand holding her coffee. Absentmindedly she had forgotten to put sweetener in it before she left the station, so it tasted like shit.

"Are you listening to me, constable?"

"Yes, ma'am."

Delores' house had gotten teepeed the night before. A bunch of kids had gathered about two dozen toilet paper rolls and mummified it. It stood looking absurd on Bartlett Avenue, covered in wet strands, sticking to the shingles and the fiber cement sidings from the morning dew.

"I tell you what, Mrs. Hamilton. It was probably that punk Greg Chandler and his buddies. I'll call a cleaning service I know in Manchester and have them help you."

"You better!" Delores took a cigarette from behind her ear and lit it between her leathery lips. It was marveling to Cole how a ninety-six-year-old woman like her could smoke as much as she did and not die. "I'm not paying to have my house cleaned. Every year, constable! You should just lock up that awful Chandler boy so he can get a taste of what's waiting for him! If Constable Graven were still here, he'd fix that boy right."

"I'll drive to his father's house and have a word with him right now."

"Good! I hope he whups that boy's ass good!"

The constable cruiser was parked on the side of the street. Cole got in and the dashboard heater soothed her. The leisure was cut short when she caught a glance of herself in the visor mirror.

*Is that...?* She leaned forward, examined herself, and then plucked a hair out of her head. It was a single gray. *Thirty-four*, she thought gloomily, *and I'm already getting grays*.

"You're looking all right, Constable Kaysen." Louis Wolfe grinned at her from the passenger seat, bemused. "Chandler kid, right?"

"The god damned Chandler kid again," Cole said, setting her coffee in the dashboard holder. "I already know it's him. We're going to stop by his dad's and talk to him."

"That'll be about the third time in two weeks, talking to him."

Just before Cole put the car into drive, a fierce sneeze escaped her face. She dug a few napkins from her coat and wiped her nose. "Before we do that, we need to head back to the station. I think I'm catching a cold, and I left my aspirin in the desk. I also need put some sweetener in this coffee. It tastes like I'm drinking tar."

"I kinda like it."

"That's because you've been chewing tobacco for half your life, Lou."

Lou chuckled. He fingered a tin from his coat pocket, sifted his thumb in it, and then dabbed some tobacco between his lower lip and gum. "Not your morning, Cole?"

"Not at all."

Lou Wolfe had been deputy constable of Leinster for around twenty-eight years. He'd lived in the village his whole life—born, raised, and likely to die in it. Most knew him personally, and some Leinsterites—such as Delores Hamilton, for example—could remember him as a little boy playing street hockey in Merrimack Square with his buddies. He was a short man, standing at about five foot five, and he had baby blue eyes that peered out of an unshaven face. Despite his receding hairline, he always kept his hair slicked back, and his raspy voice enunciated certain words with a distinctive New England twanginess that Cole felt a tug of affection for. He was a rough, old fashioned sort, but a good, honest man and a reliable deputy.

The previous constable of Leinster had been an old fart by the name of Jasper Graven. According to Lou, Jasper had been just one in a long line of Graven constables. After one son died of a drug overdose and the other was killed chasing Saddam out of Kuwait, ole Jasp had given up any hope of continuing his family line of authority in Leinster. Towards the end of his life he always had a canteen of bourbon on him and he farted about two dozen times an hour. It came as no surprise to Lou when Jasp keeled over dead of a stroke brought on from undiagnosed colon cancer in 2018.

Leinster was desperate for a new constable after Jasper died. Lou refused the title, saying that it was "too much responsibility" for a guy like him. The village board of selectmen, headed by Eddie Davenport, decided that Officer Colquitt Kaysen of the Manchester Police Department would make a good candidate. She was an experienced cop who was looking to leave the city but stay in police work. Leinster was part of Manchester, acting as a township within the city jurisdiction, so the process wasn't complicated. Cole adjusted to it well.

Leinster's constable station was a small brick building that had once been a post office, with windows shaped like old tombstones and two white pillars erected on each side of the wooden front doors. It sat across from the municipal building in Merrimack Square—the center of the village where a bronze statue of a Union soldier stood upon a concrete plinth.

The reflection of the soldier crept across the cruiser windshield like an imposing sentry as Cole pulled up and parked. "You need anything?" she asked.

Lou rolled down his window and spat a wad of tobacco on the sidewalk. "No, I'm good."

Cole got out and jogged up the front steps, digging in her pocket for the keys. Just as she mounted the last step, she stopped. A stained yellow bubble envelope lay at her feet. Scrawled on the front in what looked like charcoal was written: "FOR CONST. COLQUITT KAYSEN & LOUIS WOLFE TO OPEN IMMEDIATELY".

"Huh." Cole picked it up and then tore off the side.

Lou called from the passenger window: "Hey Cole, make it quick! Just got a call from Martha Holloway! She sounds hysterical."

Cole peeked inside the package and her body went cold. It fell from her hands. Blood and teeth sputtered out when it hit the ground.

"Cole, you all right?"

She turned to Lou, her face white as a sheet. "Lou, call Manchester now!"

The phone vibrated on the bedside table, its screen glowing in the dark room, disturbing Adrian from deep sleep. His arm slithered out from beneath the covers and snatched it. It was a 603 number, but it wasn't a number that he recognized. Did mom or Clarissa get a new number?

Lauren rolled over. "Who is it?"

Adrian pulled the phone under the covers. "Hello?"

A woman's voice: "Am I speaking with Adrian Holloway?"

"Who is this?"

"This is Constable Colquitt Kaysen from Leinster Village in Manchester. You aren't busy today, are you?"

In an instant, Adrian was wide awake. "What is it?"

"We're sorry to report that your sister and niece are missing."

"Missing?" Adrian sat up. He felt Lauren pull the covers off herself and turn to him.

"Your sister and niece went out for Halloween last night and never came home. They were last seen by your mother at around six o' clock that evening. Your mother told me that you live in Massachusetts now?"

Adrian threw his legs over the side of the bed and started pulling his boxers on. "Yeah, I've been living here for a few years."

"You should come up here, Adrian. Your mother isn't doing well."

"I'm already getting dressed. It's about an hour and a half drive. I should be in the village by around"—he eyed the clock on the wall—"noon."

"Good. See you then."

Adrian hung up. Lauren put her hand on his back. "What's happening, Adrian?

He got up and stepped into a pair of pants on the floor and pulled them up. "Clarissa and Julia—they're missing."

"What? What happened?"

"I don't know. The constable just called me saying that they went out for Halloween and never came back."

"That's horrible, Adrian."

"I need to go up there." He buttoned his pants and pulled on a shirt. "I need to see my mother. I can't imagine how she is right now."

"Do you want me to come with you?"

"No, I don't think so. You've never met my family. There's a lot about my mother that... well, it's complicated."

"What about work?"

He took his coat off the rack. "I'll tell the truth. I got a family emergency and I can't be in until it's resolved. If Chase doesn't like it, then he can kiss my ass. There are plenty of other people with less hours who can come in and run the machines."

Lauren put on some pajama bottoms with a t-shirt and walked Adrian to the front door. "I'm serious, Adrian. If you need me to come, I will."

"I'll call you tonight and let you know how things are."

"I hope they turn up okay. I'm sorry to hear all this."

"I am too."

They kissed and hugged, and then Adrian stepped outside. The door shut behind him and the locks clicked. It was cold—probably about thirty degrees. His heart was pounding so hard that he could feel it in his ears.


*Seven years*, he thought as he pulled off Exit 5 of I-93. *Doesn't feel like it's been that long since I left home.*

It had been a long time since he visited his mother and sister. Probably not since right after Julia was born. That had been Christmas about five years back. After moving to Massachusetts, he visited only occasionally, and the phone calls and texting slowly tapered off. Eventually the relationship between himself and his family was a Christmas or birthday card in the mail. There hadn't been any bitterness between himself and his family, Adrian was just caught up in work, and Clarissa had Julia. Adulthood pulled everyone away from each other. That made this already awful situation more stressful.

After crossing Michael Briggs Memorial Bridge, he entered the village. The sky was gray and there was nobody on the brick sidewalks. The shops were closed and there weren't any cars around. The village felt eerily deserted. Only the bronze Union soldier stood in Merrimack Square, his musket pointed to the sky.

Adrian drove into his old neighborhood. It was all so quaint compared to his current neighborhood in Brockton—a familiar place he knew from a past life. The houses all looked the same save for color, shrubbery and lawn decorations. The trees were stripped bare of their leaves and foliage decorated the dying yellow grass like rusty confetti. It didn't feel so nostalgic this morning.

At the end of Sanders Street, he saw the old constable cruiser parked outside his boyhood home. It was the same 1999 Ford Crown Victoria that Jasper Graven had bought after he crashed the previous cruiser into a telephone pole. The sight of it wasn't assuring. Adrian parked behind it and got out.

The old house still looked the same as he remembered it, but it was painted an ugly khaki color and the stoop had been rebuilt. *Mom must be renovating parts of the house to put value on it,* Adrian thought.

Standing on the front porch was a blonde woman in a heavy coat, fiddling on her phone. She sneezed into the bend of her arm and wiped her nose a bundle of napkins. As Adrian approached, she slipped the phone into her coat. Her nose and cheeks were red from the cold and a thick gray scarf was wrapped around her neck.

"You must be Adrian," she said, holding her hand out. "I'm Colquitt Kaysen, Leinster's constable. Just call me Cole."

He shook her hand. "You replaced Constable Graven?"

"I did. Jasp—well, he retired a few years back."

The new constable abated his anxiety. Despite her authority, there was a genuine casualness to her that Adrian really needed. Nothing like Jasper. Constable Graven always looked sullen and imposing, like he was carrying something ugly deep inside him all the time and was actively seeking ways to let it all out on somebody.

"How's my mother?"

"Not great, Adrian. I'm sure she'll appreciate your speediness. When was the last time you saw her?"

"Too long," Adrian said quietly.

"Deputy Wolfe has been with her, talking to her."

"Lou is still deputy constable?"

"He is. Go ahead and tell him I'm still out here." Cole held the door open for him.

As Adrian went to pass her, she nabbed him by the sleeve. "Adrian, not to push you in a time like this, but I need to ask if you'll be around Manchester for a while."

"I plan on staying here until my sister and niece are found."

"I see." She took a napkin from her pocket and scribbled on it with a pen. "Listen, the Manchester police are going to want to talk to you. Whenever you're ready, I ask that you come see me and Lou as well."

"I'm a suspect?"

"It's just standard procedure for a missing persons case. I'm only the constable, here to keep the peace in the village—I straighten out hooligans and domestic disputes. Missing persons is out of my hands, so the Manchester P.D. is on it. Still, I ask that you talk to me and Lou. I want to help any way that I can." She handed him the napkin. "Those are the numbers for my cell phone and the constable's office."

Adrian tucked the napkin into his coat pocket. "Thank you, constable."

"We'll get this figured out, Adrian. Life will go back to normal soon."

This old house, with its beige wallpaper, scraped up wooden floors and rickety staircase that moaned with each step taken.

On the wall by the stairs hung framed photos of Adrian and Clarissa as kids at First Communion, as well as baby photos of Julia. This house had a distinct smell Adrian never sensed while he was growing up, and only noticed now having returned after so long—old pine and dust. The scent made him feel like a teenager again, wondering when Mom would get better…

Hushed whispers came from the living room. Adrian stepped in and saw Lou sitting on a footrest next to his mother, who was in a wooden rocking chair before a window.

"Adrian Holloway." Lou said, standing. He was chewing on a toothpick. "Last I saw you, you must have been yea-big"—he held his hand to his chest.

"It's good to see that you're still around, Lou."

"For better or worse, kid." Lou slapped him on the arm and leaned to his ear. "Let's get sentimental another time. I'll leave you with your mother. Cole give you her number?"

"She did."

"Good. Call us. Those Manch cops are gonna shake you and see what falls out. Stay strong."

Lou's footsteps creaked against the floorboards as he left, and then the front door opened and shut. The house became unbearably quiet. Adrian was alone with his mother now, for the first time in over half a decade. He took a deep breath. "Mom, it's me."

Slowly, her head craned to look at him. Her eyes were set dark and deep in her alarmingly gray face. Mom never looked healthy, but now she seemed like she belonged on a slab. "Adrian?" she whispered.

"I'm here, Mom."

"They're gone, Adrian."

"I know they are." He knelt and put his hand on hers. It was ice cold, clenching the arm of the chair. "I'm staying with you until Clarissa and Julia are found."

Slowly, she rose and hugged him, burying her face into the bend of his neck. Warm tears pressed against his skin, wetting the collar of his shirt. "Adrian, where are they? I haven't been able to think all day. I just want to know that they're okay."

All the pain and anxiety within her came out at once. The sight of her wayward son unleashed the floodgates. Adrian pulled her tight, wishing somehow to take this pain from her, but he had no idea how.

It was only one o' clock and, unbeknownst to Cole or Lou, the day was far from over.

Three Manchester police cruisers were parked outside 14 Shetland Avenue. A state trooper was there too. The house was only a single floor and painted dark gray. A little pink-yellow tricycle lay abandoned on the front yard. Cops wandered the property, prodding the bushes with their batons, or shining flashlights around inside the house, their shapes moving to and fro from window to window. A fold out table was set up on the sidewalk with a coffee maker, and a Manchester cop and a state trooper were standing by it, Styrofoam cups in hand, bantering.

Cole and Lou leaned against the hood of their shabby Crown Vic, watching the investigation unfold. Both waited restlessly for any sign that would give a lead.

"It was rough, seeing Martha like that," Lou said. He had a cigarette pinched between thumb and forefinger and flicked ash off the tip with his pinky. "I mean, Martha's always been a little rough, one way or another. I went to Manchester Central High with her."

"Is that so?" Cole wasn't really listening.

"Poor girl. Growing up, she was awkward, didn't talk much and read books. Got picked on a lot because of it. I remember her pops was a boozer, and sometimes she'd come to school with these bruises." He held his wrists out for demonstration. "She seemed like the sort of girl who would blow over like a straw house if the wind was strong enough. I always wondered what her pops was hiding. You know guys who drink like that got something to hide. Why don't—"

"Lou, please. I can't listen to this right now."

Lou took a drag of his cigarette, snapped it away. "Sure. Just saying, Martha's always been a little off. I wouldn't write her off right away if she got something to do with any of this."

The trooper by the coffee maker stepped over to them. "I don't think you'll be needed for a while. If you want, you can drive up to the lab and check in on that package you received this morning.

"Sure," Cole said. The word came out like a croak. She and Lou lumbered back into the vehicle.

"You don't want to find anything out about that package, do you?" Lou said.

"You didn't see it."

This was true. She hadn't even told him about what was inside. The most he'd seen was some blood that had sputtered out of the package when Cole dropped it.

"Cole, you've been looking green about this all day. I hate to pry you about it, but—"

"It was fucking body parts, all right?"

Lou's lip quivered. "Body parts?"

"Teeth. And fleshy shit. Like organs."

"Hellfire, Cole. What organs?"

"I'm not a god damned doctor, Lou! I don't know what it was. It looked like small organs. Maybe it's just a Halloween prank or something—like maybe they're not human parts, but some animal. So soon after the Holloway mom and kid going missing, though… I don't like to think about it."

A tap came against the driver side window and Cole nearly leapt out of her skin. Grace Davenport was standing outside the cruiser—a freckled young woman with a long nose. Cole pressed a hand to her chest, feeling her heart pounding against her sternum, and then rolled the window down. "Grace, you scared the shit out of me."

"I'm sorry, Cole. I just—I heard about Clarissa and her little girl. And now I'm seeing all these cops outside her house. Is everything okay?"

*Nothing stays a secret around here for long, does it?* Cole thought grimly. "The only thing I can say is that we're looking for them."

This didn't appear assuring to Grace, and she turned her nervous gaze to the house. Cole couldn't blame her for getting spooked. Grace had a kid of her own—a seven-year-old, Jeremy. She worked at the village library down the street from the elementary school. No doubt she was thinking of him.

"Is your husband at home with Jeremy?" Cole asked.

Grace was married to Eddie Davenport, one of the village selectmen who initially vouched for Cole to become constable. Needlessly she looked fondly on the Davenport family, and she always felt like she owed them for that.

"Yes, he is. It's just so horrible. I passed by Clarissa and Julia on Jointer Avenue at around seven thirty. It just doesn't make sense that they could up and vanish like that."

"Listen Grace, go back home and stay with Eddie and your kid, all right? Tell the Manchester police what you saw, too. I can't tell you anything more, I'm sorry."

"I understand. Thank you, Cole. You too, Lou."

Grace walked off and Cole rolled up the window. After a few moments of silence, she began laughing. It started with reserved chuckles, then became bellowing guffaws.

"Cole, what's gotten into you, huh?" Lou said. He took his tin of tobacco from his coat and thumbed some brown tar behind his lip.

"I forgot all about the damn Chandler kid. God, today started out with Delores Hamilton's house getting teepeed, and now"—the laughter faded—"it's come to this. There was a reason why I left the Manchester P.D., Lou. You know it."

Lou sympathized. Cole had grown up in Manchester—grew up seeing the gambling, drugs and violent crime. Her mother getting stabbed during a home invasion was what prompted Cole to enter the police force. After a few years, she got disillusioned. Instead of making the city a better place, she was smashing car windows to Narcan dying mothers as their kids cried and screamed in the backseat. She arrested the same violent domestic abusers three times a month. Escorting the stabbed, shot and half crazed to Elliot Hospital was a daily chore. It was miserable work.

The straw that broke the policewoman's back had been a serious domestic assault late one winter night. A twenty-two-year-old addict, Raymond Sears, got high on crystal meth and cut his girlfriend up with a knife in his apartment. Cole and another officer were called in to take care of it. Ray had a rap sheet that looked like a pharmacy receipt, so she knew that it was going to be trouble. Not more than a few seconds after she and her partner broke into the apartment, Ray went after her with a needle. Cole shot him.

Ray survived but became paralyzed from the chest down, confining him to a wheelchair. His girlfriend survived as well, but she was badly disfigured. Six months later he committed suicide, a few days before he was to begin his twenty year sentence for attempted murder, assault with a deadly weapon, and assaulting a police officer. He had been staying with his parents in Londonderry at the time, and he had wheeled himself directly into the backyard swimming pool.

After that, Cole decided that she had enough of policing the city. So, she went to Leinster, where the worst she hoped for was petty vandalism and maybe a lost cat stuck in a tree.

Now there was this. Cole hadn't known Clarissa or Julia well, but she was taking their disappearance hard. Cole had a big heart, and while that sometimes had its benefits, it worked against her as well.

"You gonna be all right, Cole? You look like hell."

"I'll make it. I've got to keep my head straight."

"Don't you think—"

The dashboard radio interrupted them: "Kaysen and Wolfe?"

Cole grabbed the microphone. "Yeah, we're here."

"We got a call about vandalism in the Eternal Light Cemetery. You wanna look?"

"Sure, we're on our way." She hung up the microphone. "Started out with Delores' house getting teepeed, Lou," she said, jabbing her keys in the ignition.

The Eternal Light Cemetery wasn't far—just down the street from the Crockett Funeral Home on Waverly Avenue. It was a beautiful cemetery with wooden gazebos, a little promenade by the Merrimack River, and a stone wall with iron fencing that surrounded the property. The caretaker was a guy named Kenneth Maynard, an old friend of the cemetery's previous caretaker, Mary Shepherd. He was a greasy, bearded guy with long hair who always wore a ratty cap.

Ken stood outside the cemetery gates, smoking a cigarette and scratching his scalp through his hat. When the Crown Vic pulled up, he snapped his cigarette away and waltzed up to Cole and Lou as they got out.

"Got some creepy shit going on here, Constable Kaysen," he said.

"Trust me, it's probably not as creepy as the shit I saw this morning," Cole said.

The constables followed Ken into the cemetery, passing the angel statues, crypts, and crooked headstones.

"I didn't see this until about an hour ago," Ken explained. "I was about to start mowing when I found it."

"Well, what the hell is it, Ken?" Lou asked.

They approached a lone plot towards the back of the cemetery. The grave had a rectangular, nondescript headstone, with a single name engraved upon it: PETER BELLE.

Tobacco dripped off Lou's chin. "Shit," he whispered.

Chunks of semi-frozen soil littered the ground around a sinkhole in front of the headstone. The ground sagged inward. Cole knelt, pressed her fingertips against the dry grass, then knotted her fingers through it and pulled up a portion of earth like a small carpet. Beneath was a big hole of loose dirt, torn up roots, and rocks.

"What is it?" Lou peered over her shoulder. "Vandalism?"

"I don't know."

Cole wanted to believe that it was vandalism, but it didn't seem like it. It looked like something beneath the ground had emerged to the surface.


"Were you ever close?"

Adrian was in his old bedroom, pacing back and forth while on the phone with Laruen. In the years since he left the village, his mother had converted it into a storeroom. Bent and dusty carboard boxes were stacked in the corners and the air was musky. Mom managed to get an air mattress out of the hall closet and set it up on the floor for Adrian.

It was a question he had to consider for some time before answering. "Yeah," Adrian said. "I mean, we haven't been close in recent years. We grew apart after I moved and especially after Clarissa had Julia. It was nothing personal. We just had lives that were going in different directions. When we were young, we were close. I'm feeling a little regretful now."

"Why?"

"I just feel like I should have at least tried to reach out more. I should have come up to visit more often."

"I know it's hard, but you can't beat yourself up right now. You need to stay strong until they're found."

"I know."

"Was she seeing anybody? Where's Julia's father?"

"That's a long story. Clarissa met this guy from Massachusetts, and they got married too soon. After she had Julia, the guy wouldn't get a full-time job and was buying all this arbitrary shit with borrowed money—car parts and booze mostly. The marriage fell through when Clarissa went through his phone one night and saw that he was seeing somebody. They divorced and she got custody. Clarissa's been a single mom since. The guy wasn't much different from my dad, honestly."

"That's rough. What about your mom?"

"What about her?"

"Well, are you close to her? I know you said your dad left, but you never talked about your mom much."

"It's complicated. After Dad left, Mom was a wreck. She suffered this nervous breakdown that lasted for years. My sister, she was about ten at the time, and she took it upon herself to raise me. Mom was out of work—she'd be on the couch for hours at a time surrounded by tissues with the TV on mute. It was an ugly thing. She couldn't cook, couldn't go out for errands. There were periods where she was institutionalized—at Robynsville first, then later at Hampstead Hospital. My sister cooked for me, bought me clothes, walked with me to school. Clarissa took charge when there was no one else there for us, and she was only ten years old. She needed parenting too, but she carried both of us while Mom struggled to get back on her feet. I was always grateful to her for that."

"It sounds like your sister is a strong woman, Adrian."

"That's why it's so complicated. The relationship between my mother and sister has been strained ever since. Mom didn't get herself together until Clarissa was almost sixteen. In all that time, she really needed a parent, and Mom wasn't there. Instead, she was parenting me. My sister has this very... civil relationship with my her. Mom beats herself up a lot over it, blames herself for a lot of Clarissa's problems, and my sister tries to understand and be sympathetic about it, but I think there's a part of her that resents her. Clarissa visits her, but I think she keeps Mom at arm's length. I don't know how things are between them now, but when I left Leinster that's how it was."

"That's awkward."

"And now she and my niece are missing."

"What about you, Adrian?"

"Honestly? I just want to find them. Ever since I got that phone call, I can't stop thinking about how fucked up this family is. How we're all so far apart from one another. And it's made me realize that I haven't appreciated my family enough. I'm scared, Lauren. I want us all to just be okay. I want us to stop being so estranged from one another." He scoffed. "I just want them back. I swear, if they're found, then I'll do everything to try and bring everyone together again. I should have before."

"Are you sure you don't want me to come up?"

For a moment, he considered it. "No, I don't think so. I think it's best if I stay here, just me and my mother."

"I understand. Listen, call me whenever you get a chance, okay? Keep me updated on everything."

"Thanks, babe. I'll talk to you later."

"Goodnight."

He hung up and gazed out the window to the sky. The moon shined in the black night. What was this phase called again? First quarter? The moon wasn't something he actively paid attention to, but it did seem a little strange that the cycles were moving quicker than usual.

It was surreal being here again. Despite the boxes and the decrepit feel of the room, there were hints of an old life that lingered. There was a scar on the wall from Adrian punching it when he was fourteen, and there were still traces of tape from old band posters on the ceiling over where his bed used to be. In the closet, a little heart with "A.H. + J.W." was carved in the floorboards—his first serious girlfriend Jennifer Watkins in high school. In the far left corner remained a couple of dye stains from when he splattered a t-shirt for an art project.

If a stranger stepped in here, it would have the outward appearance of being nothing more than a junk room where things were put to be forgotten. If one were to pull back the intricacies of the room, they would find evidence that someone had existed.

Adrian felt compelled to go to the room across the hall. He stepped out and stood before the wooden door, feeling butterflies of anxiety bounce around in his abdomen. His hand raised, and his fingertips drummed against the door, and then he gently pushed it open.

This had been Clarissa's room. Not a large room by any means—large enough for only a single window. It was an office now. Mom's desk and computer were in the corner where Clarissa's bed used to be. The only thing of Clarissa's that remained was the polished mahogany bookshelf. It wasn't filled with young adult fantasy and science fiction that she enjoyed as a teenager, but with Mom's art and history books.

As a little kid, when Mom was asleep, Adrian would creep across the hall and his sister would let him in her room. Into the early hours of the morning, he and his sister would talk. About Dad, and all the horrible ways he used to make them feel. About love, and what it all meant. About the future, and all the things they dreamed of being. Adrian had told her once that he wanted to be a movie director, and Clarissa had replied that she never planned on getting married or having kids, and wanted to have an art studio in Brooklyn.

*Funny how the years change us*, Adrian thought. He never wound up directing any movies, and the closest Clarissa had ever been to Brooklyn was Jersey City for a concert.

Adrian felt his throat tighten, and he had to close the door. It was too much, to look in on this room.

In the kitchen, Martha Holloway sat alone at the table. A cigarette was burned down to the filter between her fingers. The tray by her hand was overflowing with crumbled and half spent butts. Smoke lingered in the air within the light hanging over the kitchen table, and Martha's face was half cast in shadow. Beer cans littered the table along with a half empty bottle of liquor.

"Mom," Adrian said as he stepped in.

Martha seemed to awaken from her trance, and she swiped ash off the table with her sleeve and crushed the butt out in the tray. "It's been twenty-four hours now, officially. Since I realized that your sister was late getting back."

"Mom, stop."

"No." She took a fresh cigarette and lit up. "I was a terrible mother."

"You weren't a terrible mother. You just had problems."

"Don't play dumb, Adrian. I wasn't there when your sister needed me. I wasn't there when you needed me. I was so wrapped up in my own shit—in your father. And now they're gone."

"Mom, what Dad did to you was unfair. It was unfair to all of us. You needed help. It's not your fault."

"Yes it is!" She slapped her hand to the table. "I am your mother, Adrian. I'm supposed to protect you and your sister. I remember it all. I can still see your sister coming to me while I was in bed, shaking me and asking when I was going to come back—that you were both starving. And I did nothing but lay there. Memories like that linger with me every day, pushing me to be the best mother I could after I got myself together. But I missed half a decade for you guys. I never said it out loud because I knew that you and Clarissa would just say, 'Oh no, mom, it's okay,' and downplay it. Everything about my relationship with your sister is forced—right down to when I saw her last, when she came to this house last night before she went trick or treating."

The tears came as she talked. "Do not try and tell me that it's all right, Adrian. I thought I could make up for it somehow, to be an amazing grandmother to Julia, but I could feel your sister keeping her at a distance from me. And now they're both gone. How can I not condemn myself?"

Now she was sobbing. Adrian watched her impotently. It was all true. He never had a relationship with her, but she was still his mother. The love he had for her would have been something completely different, something more intense, had she been present in his upbringing, but that didn't mean that he didn't love her at all.

"Mom, you need to get a grip on yourself. Okay? My sister and niece—your daughter and granddaughter—they're still out there. They need you to be strong. If you want to prove your love to either of them, then you can start now. Stop with the drinking and the smoking. We *will* find them."

Martha pulled her hands from her face. She still looked haggard, but she nodded. "Yes," she said.

Adrian hugged her. When they let go, Martha saw that her fresh cigarette had gone out. Slowly, she slipped it back into the pack.

"It's only a matter of time before the search parties begin," Adrian went on. "I've been told that the Manchester police will want to question us soon. You need to be sober for that."

"Right."

"And you need to rest."

"I'll be in bed shortly."

"Good. I'll be in my old room if you need me."

Adrian made his way to the doorway. Martha's voice stopped him: "I probably should have seen this coming."

"Huh? What did you say?"

She was picking at the filters in her pack of smokes. "Have you noticed the moon?"

"What about it?"

"It's been passing through the lunar cycles. Faster than normal. Sometimes… it's not our decision that these things happen. Sins of the father—we're all accounted for because of them."

"What the hell are you talking about, Mom?"

She waved it off. "It's nothing, honey. I'm drunk. I'm a mess. I don't know what I'm saying."

Adrian didn't press it further and stepped out. He was too tired to think about it. Within minutes of lying down, he was asleep.

# November 2nd

# Waxing Gibbous

"**K**idneys."

Cole felt her heart skip a beat. "Run that by me again?"

Chief Medical Examiner of Hillsborough County, Ephrem Jessup, stood washing his hands at the steel sink in the coroner examination room. It was a discomfortingly sterile room that Cole didn't like being in. A porcelain slab stood between Jessup and the constables, and the air was so cold that they could see their breath.

"Kidneys?" Lou said. "Like—"

"Human." Jessup turned the faucet off and shook his hands off over the sink, then nabbed a paper towel from the dispenser nearby. He was a chubby man with a faint voice. "Two of them. One from an adult woman and the other from a child, a girl probably between the ages of four and six. That's what was delivered to your door yesterday morning. Along with human teeth."

"Fuck me," Cole wheezed. "How the—why?"

"I know this may be difficult to hear."

"That's an understatement," Lou said. "Cole, we gotta start with the search parties now. Get Eddie on the horn. Keep this between you and me for now. Get the whole board at the town hall now. We have to find them."

The first bell rung out. The children in classroom 313 of Leinster Village Elementary stood almost in unison—dozens of chair legs *scrrrrch*ing against the tiled floor—and put their chairs up on the tables upside down. At the sound of the second bell, they rushed out of the class and crowded into the hallways.

Among the children was a thin, bright haired boy with gray eyes. He sported a denim coat and glasses, as well as shoes with heels that lit up with each step he took. The children lined up outside at their assigned buses, and the boy was passing through the east parking lot towards them when a name called out for him.

"Jeremy!"

The boy stopped, looked around, and then saw his mother next to her red van at the edge of the lot. She waved and smiled, signaling him to come over.

Jeremy trotted over to her, struggling to keep the straps of his backpack from falling off his shoulders. "Hi Mom!"

"Hey sweetheart." She got on her knees and kissed him.

"What are you doing here?"

"Oh—I have an early break today. Things at the library are slow, so I thought I'd pick you up from school."

"But I always take the bus home."

"Well, about that"—she stood and opened the passenger door—"hop in. I'd like to tell you something."

They got in and the car pulled onto Pierce Street. Jeremy Davenport watched the little brick building get smaller in the side mirror. All his friends took the bus home, and since he didn't share any classes with them, the bus ride to and from school was the only time he got to be with them.

Mom looked anxious. She drummed her fingers on the steering wheel. "Jeremy," she began, "I don't—look, it's like… well, it's—"

"What's going on, Mom?"

"The flu. Yes, there's a new flu going around town. West Nile, it comes from the flies. It's going through all the schools in Manchester."

"I didn't see anyone sick in class today."

"I'd like you to do something for me over the next few days. After you get out of class, I will pick you up and drive you home. I'll also drive you to school in the morning, so you don't have to walk to the bus stop down the street."

"I only ever get to see my friends on the bus."

"I know, sweetie. I'm sorry. You can't afford to miss any school days. Another thing, your father is going out for an important meeting today with the board of selectmen. He'll be leaving not long after I drop you off. I want you to stay inside."

"But why?"

"Because!" She struggled to answer. "I just want you to stay inside, okay? And lock the doors as well."

They made it home. Grace parked the car as far up as she could in the driveway and got out with her son. "I'm sorry for doing this, hun. It's really important."

Eddie Davenport was pacing in the living room, anxiously twirling a pen between his fingers. He was a lanky man who wore a pair of round glasses that always sat at the bottom of his nose. His hair was loose in a handsome, boyish sort of way over his forehead, and it combed over nicely whenever he ran his fingers through it. The moment Grace and Jeremy walked in, he ceased his pacing and went over to them.

"Oh good! Jeremy!" He picked the child up and held him. "Good to see you home. Did your mother already talk to you?"

The boy nodded.

Eddie kissed him on the forehead and set him down. "Listen Jeremy, your mother and I need to talk really quick, okay? Could you run to your room for a bit?"

Jeremy did so. He went down the hall and his bedroom door shut. Grace and Eddie were alone and the atmosphere in the room became heavy.

"When are you going to Merrimack Square?" Grace asked.

"I'm leaving as soon as Jeremy is settled in. You going back to the library?"

"I have to. It's just Susan right now. Eddie, are they going out looking for them?"

"That's what we're organizing." He took his coat from the rack near the front door and slipped it on. "We're having a few officers from Manchester sit in on the meeting. It's going to be me, Mickey Collins, Constables Kaysen and Wolfe, and the other selectmen."

"Do you think it's serious?" Grace shifted from foot to foot like she always did when she was high strung. "What if something horrible happened to them?"

"We don't know that, Grace." He zipped up his coat and put his hands on her shoulders. "It could be anything. I'm hoping that maybe Clarissa just decided to split town or something."

"It's just—seeing all those cop cars outside her house. It got me scared, you know? Just the idea that someone—I can't even think about it."

"You told Jeremy to stay indoors, right?"

"And to keep the doors locked. But I still don't like leaving him here alone."

"I can call my sister. She can come over and watch him."

Eddie could feel the physical tension in his wife's shoulders ease. "That would make me feel better."

"I can do that right now, okay? But I can't wait much longer. I have to get to that meeting."

"Go ahead."

He kissed her, and then took his phone from his pocket. "We may get started with the search soon, and I'm not sure when I'll be back. I'll call Annie on my way out and she'll be here in fifteen minutes, then you can head back to the library."

"Thank you."

He opened the front door, dialed his sister and pressed the phone to his ear. Before he closed the door, he looked at Grace and gave her an assuring smile. Even in her state of mind, it managed to pick her up a bit. Twenty minutes later, Annie arrived and Grace left.

The library on Pierce Street was a little colonial brick building that had once been the home of the Miller family—

Leinster's old line of mayors before the village became part of Manchester. It had bright red bricks and a white front door. A black iron chimney sprouted from its steep gables like a mushroom. It looked like something out of a Hawthorne yarn.

The inside of the library resembled the old house it had once been, with an anteroom, living room and kitchen, all restored with each room representing books of all kind—fiction, nonfiction, religious, special studies and so on. Most of the furniture and appliances in these rooms had been removed, except for old chairs and couches for guests to relax on.

At the reception desk near the front door, an older woman with graying black hair and overdone makeup was scanning books into the library computer—a sad old thing from 2006 with a box monitor. Her name was Susan Teller.

The bell over the front door chimed and Grace stepped in. Susan looked up from the screen. "Did everything go all right, Grace?"

"As well as it could go. Jeremy is at home. Eddie's sister is watching him while he's out with the board of selectmen about the search parties." She went around the desk to a pushcart filled with books. Grace began aggressively organizing the books on it alphabetically. "I just need to not think about any of this right now, Susan. I need to stay busy."

"It might be that the mother is trying to get the child away from a bad home, is all. Get away from a bad husband."

"Clarissa hasn't had a man in her life for years, Susan. Look, I don't see anything wrong with being a little extra careful until this whole disappearance thing cools down."

"You'll be leaving early then?"

"No, I need to work."

Susan watched Grace for a few moments. The young mother's hands were shaking and her eyes anxiously darted from one book to the next.

Susan Teller was Leinster's old librarian. For over forty years, she ran this establishment, and she had watched Grace grow up. As a young girl, Grace would come to the library after school and would spend hours at a time in the old anteroom reading book after book. Her childhood was filled with stories about Narnia, Hobbits and big, hulking three-legged alien machines. Most of the books she read were recommended to her by Susan herself. And now here Grace was, a thirty-year-old woman, scanning and shelving some of the very books she had read over twenty years ago. Susan cared about her deeply. It wounded her to see her so shaken and aghast.

"You look awful, Grace," Susan told her.

"I know."

"I can let you have some time off."

"Susan!" Grace raised her voice. "I need to stay busy. Please. Just let me work. I'll feel better when Clarissa and Julia are home safe. Okay? Until then, I can't think about it."

Susan considered this, and then sighed. "I understand," she said. She turned back to the computer and scanned another book.

Mom and Dad were fighting again. No, it wasn't a fight really. It was just Mom. It was always Mom, especially when she was drinking.

"What makes you think you could come home so soon?"

Amy Gillespie lay on her bed in her little grungy room, with its stained walls and carpet, drawing pictures in her notebook. She tried to ignore her mother, but her voice rattled the walls. One way or another, Mom found a way to make the whole house poisonous to be in.

"We got bills to pay, you know!" Mom shouted. She'd been drinking from that handle of rum in the cabinet since around nine that morning.

"I need to be home for Amy," Dad said. "I keep hearing all these rumors about the Holloway kid and her mom—that Constable Kaysen and Lou got a package with blood in it or something after they went missing. I can't leave Amy—"

"Can't leave Amy what? What are you trying to say, Samuel?"

"I'm not saying anything."

"And what's the matter with having Amy here with me, eh? While you're at work? Why do you need to be here?"

"Because—I just—"

"Are you calling me a bad mother?"

Amy heard it then, the loud smack that she recognized as her mother hitting her father. Her body clenched up at the sound of the impact. The pen she'd been using to draw with fell from her hand and she pressed her palms against her ears.

"Don't you raise your voice at me, you piece of shit. You call me a bad mother when you leave work early when you know that we need the money. You are a fucking insult of a father to our child. You got something to say to me, big man?"

"You only want me to work so you can max out our credit cards."

A few more smacks. Amy flinched with each one of them. The sound of them seeped through her hands and into her ears.

"Big fuckin' man talking down to a woman like that, huh? Samuel?"

"Frances, stop."

"Shut up!"

Amy couldn't take it anymore. She rolled off her bed, went to her window and opened it. She crawled through the window and into the backyard. It was the only way to get out of the house without witnessing the scene unfolding between her parents. She knew her parents were in the living room, and to get to either the front or back doors, she would have had to pass through it.

It was still the afternoon and there was plenty of daylight. It was always melancholy around these New England Novembers. Everything seemed to fade before dying as the winter closed in. The days got shorter and the dark grew stronger. Mom's voice was still present, echoing from the house, but it was muffled now and less distinct. It was the best Amy could hope for.

The home in which she lived—a single floor mobile home that stood crooked on uneven foundations—had a small yard in the back. At the edge of the yard were woods. Leaves rolled like little yellow and red tumbleweeds along the lawn in the chilly breeze. Hanging from the only tree in the yard was a swing that her father had made her from two chains and a piece of plywood. It wasn't much, but it meant a lot to her.

She went to the swing and sat on it, gripping the cold chains as she rocked herself back and forth with the toe of her shoe against the dirt. For a while she cried, reflecting on that day's events.

Greg Chandler and his awful friend Aaron had made fun of the way she smelled and how frazzled her hair was on the playground that morning. Aaron had grabbed her hair and Greg had spat in her face, then stole her hairpin and stomped on it. Amy knew that she smelled bad and that her clothes were dirty. There hadn't been any soap in the house for weeks. Amy was pale and gaunt, and her clothes were too small for her and covered in stains. It was because of Mom's partying and drinking—there wasn't much money around after she got a hold of it.

This sort of bullying was something she kept buried inside herself. She couldn't tell her mother, because telling her anything would just make Mom twist the experience around to be about herself. And Dad? She trusted him and knew that she could tell him anything, but the idea of burdening him with her problems after he had worked twelve hours was something that she wasn't comfortable with.

Thinking of all this embittered her. Enraged, Amy got off the swing and grabbed a rock. She pitched the rock into the woods at the edge of the yard.

*I just want to run away!* she thought. *I wish I could just take Dad and run away from Mom forever!*

The woods ahead suddenly seemed appealing. She just wanted to be away from this house that didn't feel like home, even if it was just for a few hours. The woods seemed to her like an escape from Mom, her house, third grade, Greg Chandler, how ugly she was, and everything else.

Amy ran into the woods. It didn't matter what direction she went in. Mom's voice being far away from her was the only thing that mattered. On she went, jumping over rocks, dodging trees, until she was deep enough in to be in total silence.

It was meditating and soothing to be alone here. Somewhere far off she heard a woodpecker rattling its beak against a tree, and the sound of running water. She walked, kicking leaves, until she found herself at a small stream. It was clear, and she could see the pebbles and rocks beneath the flowing water. Amy took off her shoes and stepped in, allowing the water to crawl around her ankles. The current tickled her.

It was in this moment of clarity and peace, that she noticed several wooden planks nailed into the dirt between an opening in the trees ahead. Amy stepped out of the stream, dried her feet with her socks, put her shoes back on, and ventured to the opening.

The planks made up a trail venturing down a hill. At the bottom of the hill were what looked like the remains of an old house. Brick foundations stood in the clearing at the end of the path, with pillars stacked in a rectangular symmetry. A stone staircase, covered in vines and discolored from age, wound up in a half spiral, leading to nowhere. Pine needles and leaves carpeted the site. It resembled ancient ruins from some Tolkien fable.

A smile crept across Amy's mouth and she approached the site in wonder.

The first thing she did was examine an old steel and brick fireplace. Its chimney stood, half crumbled, about four feet tall. She got on her knees and peered inside. There was an old rat nest within, and it stank of damp water. Then she went to the staircase and began to ascend it. She had to be careful, as the steps were slippery, and some of them were so steep that she had to climb up onto them. Once she neared the top, she felt as if she were queen of the universe. The view of the forest was clear all around. She could see the stream, the hill, a large granite formation emerging from the earth like some mythical giant, and even an old rusty firetruck.

There was something else too, though. Smoke rose in pillowing gray clouds from the ground a few yards ahead. Carefully, Amy descended the stairs and went over to it.

It was a small bonfire that looked to have been recently put out. White stones encircled a blackened pit of orange embers and burned wood. In front of the bonfire was some sort of scarecrow made up of branches and sticks. Upon the sticks was an old ratty costume, smeared with black soot and dirt, and something else too. Something brown. A red hair ribbon was propped up on another stick where a head would be. It looked like a costume—a Snow White costume.

Amy's eyes went down to the fire pit again. There was something else in there. Something burning that wasn't wood or coal. Part of her wanted to examine it further, but instinct held her back. She started to back away.

A strong gust of wind blew by. The scarecrow swayed with it, and somewhere out there in those woods, she thought she could hear a voice. Amy didn't like it here anymore. She ran.

At no point did she look back as she fled. She ran up the path, nearly stumbling over, and followed the stream.

In the distance, she could hear her name being called. "Amy!"

Amy stopped in her tracks, terrified. Another breeze chilled her.

"Amy!"

The voice—she recognized it. It was her father. She ran, following it. "Dad! I'm here!" she called. All she cared about now was getting out of these woods. "Here!"

"Amy? Where are you?"

"Dad! I'm coming!"

She could see her house through the trees, and she stumbled into the backyard. Her father was on the other side of the yard, calling into the woods. A cigarette burned between his fingers and he was still wearing his work jumpsuit with "DILLON AUTO REPAIR" imprinted on the back.

"Right here, Dad!" she ran to him.

Terror was in his eyes. He pitched the cigarette away and flew to her, grabbing her jacket and checking her neck.

"Dad—"

"Where did you go?"

"I just went into the woods, where the water was."

"Are you hurt?"

"Dad, what's the big deal?"

Dad knelt before her and he clenched her arms tight enough for it to hurt. His frightened eyes were discomforting to look directly into. "Amy, I don't want you running off alone like that," he said with audible restraint in his voice. "Do you understand?"

"Dad, I—"

"Do you understand?"

Amy felt a lump developing in her throat, but fear kept her tears at bay. "Yes."

"Don't ever wander off where I can't see you. You're too important, Amy."

Dad's expression went soft, and now he looked as if he himself were about to cry. He kissed her and hugged her. "I'm sorry, sweetie. I just got scared."

Amy said nothing, but silently she forgave him.

Dad picked her up and carried her back into the house. Mom was passed out in the bedroom, so things were okay for now. She considered telling him what she had found in the woods but decided not to. The only thing that mattered now was that they had the house to themselves while Mom was asleep. He put on one of her favorite movies, sat her down in the recliner, and then began making her dinner.

The Leinster Village municipal building, where town meetings were held, had once been a small but exquisite theater. It had a traditional proscenium stage, red cushioned theater seats, and velvet blue curtains. It had hosted a few notable productions before it was shut down in 1929, notably *The Dark Lady of the Sonnets*, *The Fascinating Widow*, and *Mary Magdalene*. The Wall Street Crash had been the kiss of death to it. It sat dormant on Merrimack Square for years, and after a new theater was built in the city, Mayor Josephat T. Benoit talked about demolishing it. The citizens of Leinster voted for the building to stay, and collectively funded to have it renovated into a town hall.

The village had two head selectmen: Edward Davenport and Mickey Collins. There had been a third, Stuart Mayfair, but he died back in July after having a heart attack while swimming at Hampton Beach. The village council also included the constable and her deputy, as well as the village clerk and a few independent businesses.

The council got together and discussed how the night would proceed for about a half hour. Once wrapped up, about two dozen people emerged from the municipal building and gathered around the bronze Union soldier in the center of Merrimack Square. Several Manchester police officers were present as well. It was close to three thirty in the afternoon, but there were still a few hours of daylight.

Everyone was muttering to each other in hushed tones. The general consensus among the crowd was mixed.

"They've got to be dead."

"That mom probably went crazy and stole the kid."

"Did you hear? Colquitt and Lou got blood delivered to their doorstep not long after the Holloways went missing."

Others stayed optimistic, assuring one another that Clarissa and her daughter would turn up somehow. Nobody had all the answers, so nobody could conclude any motive or the fate of Clarissa and Julia.

Martha Holloway rubbed her hands together and watched the sky. She had herself mostly together by this point, because seeing so many people in the village band together to help her family did wonders for her morale. However, there was still an aura of oppression that loomed over her, and her mind more often than not wandered into dark and terrible places.

Adrian put a hand on her shoulder. "Mom, are you going to be all right doing this?"

"Look at that."

"What?"

She pointed. "The moon."

Even in the afternoon, the moon still lingered prominently in the sky.

"God," Martha shook her head. "It's waxing gibbous… it looks like it's already moving on to the next phase already. It's not natural."

"Mom, I asked you a question."

The moon's hypnotism over Martha broke. She blinked and looked at her son morosely. "Yes. I'll be fine. I'm sorry, this is all just a little overwhelming. I need to do this." She slipped a cigarette into her mouth and lit it. Her voice faint and shaken. "I have to be here. I owe your sister."

A whistle silenced the crowd. Next to the bronze soldier, Eddie Davenport stood on a bench. "Everyone! I want to thank you all for coming. Mayor Craig is aware of the search parties we've organized and has offered to have the Manchester Police Department help us. We will be divided into five separate groups to cover different parts of the village, each headed by a separate police officer. We have a lot of ground to cover. Line up, and Mickey Collins and I will organize the groups."

Adrian and Martha were grouped up with five other people—all of whom Adrian didn't know, but Martha seemed familiar with. Cole was grouped with them as well, and Eddie told them to search the hilly fields by the river, near the old sugar house where Geoff Kindless used to live.

Cole approached Adrian and Martha with a big flashlight dangling from one hand and a coffee in the other. Heavy purple bags hung under her eyes.

"You seem tired, Constable Kaysen," Adrian told her, trying to lighten the mood.

Cole chuckled morbidly. "It's been a hell of a few days, Adrian."

Once everyone was organized, Eddie whistled. "One last thing, people! Each police officer assigned to your group has a radio. If any one of you finds anything, you are to tell him immediately!"

Something flew over Cole's head. A huge raven sailed over the crowd, and then it perched itself on a branch above the square. It seemed to scan everyone like some watch tower sentry at the center of a panopticon.

"That's a damn big bird," Cole remarked.

The bird fluttered off the branch, then settled on the bronze soldier's hat. As Eddie Davenport continued addressing the crowd, people took notice of the bird. Some pointed at it. Its head twitched, and then it flew off again.

"Is that clear?" Eddie said.

There were shouts and calls of acknowledgement from the crowd. The groups started to disperse. The cigarette in Martha's mouth had gone out, but she didn't notice. Her hands were clutched together and pressed against her chest.

Eddie approached. "Martha," he said, pushing his glasses up his nose. "I know we don't know each other well."

"I know your wife at the library," Martha said without looking at him.

"I just want you to know that it's brave of you to come out here tonight. If you need anything at all, please don't hesitate to radio me. I know you're in hell right now."

"Thank you, Eddie. Really."

Unbeknownst to everyone, the raven had now settled on the rain gutter of the municipal building. It took note of how many people were there, and in what directions they were going. Satisfied, it flew away.

Deep into the night, lights from dozens of flashlights cut through the dark all over Leinster, searching bridges, alleys and fields. The raven circled above, keeping a close eye on things. Eventually, it flew south, towards the Litchfield border, to its master. It settled on the decrepit fireplace of the old ruins in the woods. Angelique took in what the bird had seen.

Carefully, she planned her next move.

# November 3rd
# Full Moon

It was a groggy morning. Rain pooled along the sides of the streets, conjuring a spectral mist that lingered throughout the village. Craig Campbell's SUV patrolled the neighborhoods, and Craig shuffled out at every stop to jog across the yards and streets to toss the morning paper onto each stoop.

At around seven, Craig finished his route on Garett Street, and then proceeded down Shetland Avenue. He was only a third of the way through his deliveries and his back was already killing him. It was his weight, he knew. He had hoped that delivering papers would help with that, but hadn't helped much at all. By this point every morning he just wanted to go home, get drunk and pass out for the rest of the day.

He stopped the SUV and struggled out of the driver seat, then trotted up the lawn of 13 Shetland Avenue and pitched a newspaper at the stoop. It hit the front door and plopped messily onto the welcome mat.

"Good enough," Craig said.

Once he caught his breath, he ran off the lawn and crossed the street. He took about three strides onto the lawn of 14 Shetland Avenue before stopping. He froze like some amateur sculpture of an obese Olympian. The paper dropped from his fingers and he could feel his heart plunge into his gut. For several moments he was unable to comprehend what he was seeing. A leftover Halloween decoration? A prank? On some instinctive level, he knew that this was neither.

Crucified to a tree on the front lawn was the headless cadaver of a woman. It was bloated green and covered in ants and maggots. Five long knives were pierced through its body.

Around the time Craig was phoning Constable Kaysen, Adrian woke up and went downstairs to the kitchen. There, his mother was anxiously scanning each page of the morning paper.

"Mom, when was the last time you ate something?"

"I don't remember," she replied through the paper.

Adrian took a pan from the sink and set it on the stove. "Let me make you some eggs."

"Honey, you don't have to do that."

"I will. You need to eat."

Within fifteen minutes he set a small plate of scrambled eggs on the table before his mother. They chatted for a bit, about the weather, the Red Sox, and so on. With a steaming cup of coffee, Adrian returned to his old room upstairs and called his girlfriend.

Not more than five minutes passed before he heard it. It began as a low hoarse bellow, followed by a pause, and then became a shrill, whistling cry. It struck Adrian like lightning. Never had he heard Mom like this, not even when Dad left. It meant only one thing. His phone fell from his hand and he felt his chest go hollow.

In the foyer, Martha Holloway was on her knees, grabbing her throat, choking. Lou Wolfe was standing before her. The look on his face was of excruciating helplessness. A Manchester cop knelt next to her, trying to talk to her.

For the rest of the afternoon, the neighbors around the Holloway house were not spared the grief. As they showered, cooked, or spent time with their children, they could hear Martha's hysterical wailing. They knew what it meant.

The Crown Vic pulled up to the constable's office and parked. Inside, Cole heard its engine shut off, followed by the front door opening and shutting. She sat with her boots up on the desk, getting her paperwork and folders dirty and wet. Her hands were laced together in her lap, and her eyes stared at nothing.

The office door opened and Lou stepped in, looking haggard and raw. He went over to the coffee maker, took the kettle off and started drinking straight out of it.

"Fuck, he grunted. "That was the worst thing I've ever seen."

"You weren't there, Lou," Cole whispered. "You didn't see it for yourself."

Lou wiped his mouth with his sleeve and rubbed the back of his neck. "I know. Seeing Martha like that—that was hard. But you? I'm sorry you saw what you did."

Lou had slept in that morning, so Cole had gotten Craig Campbell's call. It had been Cole who saw Clarissa Holloway decapitated and crucified to a tree in front of her house.

Cole brought her feet down, leaned forward and put her hands against her face. "Lou, I don't know what we're going to do."

"What can we do? It's gone up the ladder. This isn't just a missing persons case anymore. It's homicide. The state and the city gotta deal with it now."

"I didn't know Clarissa well. I saw her around town, but I never really spoke to her. I watched Julia perform in *The Wizard of Oz* at her school, when the principal asked me to help with the event. She was one of those flying monkeys."

"Cole, we haven't found Julia yet."

She shot him a venomous glare. "Don't try and bullshit me, Lou. They're both dead." Tears rolled down her face, and she snatched a handful of tissues from the box near her keyboard and wiped her face.

Lou sat down at his desk, rubbing his forehead with his fingertips. "You didn't see anything?"

"See what? The fucking dead woman with no head nailed to a tree?"

"I know it's gotta be hard, but did you see any details?"

"I saw some details, Lou. It wasn't pleasant."

Lou shut up. Awkwardly, he started doodling on his notepad.

"But," Cole muttered, "knives."

"Huh?"

"There were knives." She dropped her tissues. "Seven of them. They were long ones, at least fourteen inches, like those butcher knives."

"Cimeter knives? Our killer is a butcher?"

"That's what the Manchester police think. But don't you think it's unusual to leave murder weapons around, especially with the body? Either the killer wants to be caught, or the knives were put there deliberately."

"What are you getting at?"

"There were seven knives total. Five were"—her voice cracked—"five were in the body. But there were two others. They were sticking out of the ground next to the tree, with the handles pointed towards the sky. It's a message."

"What message? What are you on about, Cole?"

"It's a Tarot, Lou."

"A what?"

Cole stood and went to the window. "Five of swords. It's a Tarot card. On it, there's this picture of a thief stealing five swords, then looking back at two he left behind. Upright, it means injustice or betrayal. Like someone committed a wrong and got away with it."

"That's a pretty big fuckin stretch, Cole."

"No—it was deliberate, if you know anything about Tarot. Why put five knives in the body and then stick two in the ground directly next to it, upright with one another?"

"How the hell do you know all this?"

"I went through a phase in high school."

"I still think it's bullshit, Cole. You're looking too deep into things. You gotta rest. You saw some traumatic shit this morning and your head isn't screwed on all the way."

Cole dug a bottle of aspirin from her desk, popped the cap and downed a few. Then she took her coat off her chair and slipped it on.

"Cole, where do you think you're going?"

"Lou, I need you to visit the coroner. Can you do that this afternoon?"

"They probably won't let me anywhere near the coroner until at least tomorrow."

"Try today. I've got to speak to Adrian."

"Uh yeah, I'd wait on that." Lou stood and held his hand up. "I'd give the Holloways some time to themselves. The last thing they need right now is more lawmen questioning them. The city cops were already pushing them hard after we told Martha the news."

"I'm not sure if there's time. I just need to speak with Adrian, preferably as soon as possible. That's all."

"Well, when the hell should I expect you back, Cole?"

"You got a phone, don't you?"

Lou groaned. "Fine."


It was getting to be evening. The house on 6 Sanders Street sat hidden in the dark. Every other house around it had some lights on in the windows, but not a single light could be seen in the Holloway house. It seemed like it just wanted to disappear. Had it not been for the full moon's light, the house wouldn't have been visible at all.

Cole parked her cruiser on the side of the road across from the house. For several moments she contemplated on how to go about this. How exactly do you approach someone at a time like this? A six pack of beer sat in the passenger seat. It must have been getting warm, with how long Cole was putting this off.

"Fuck it," she said, grabbing the beer by the plastic rings. She got out of the vehicle and knocked on the front door. The wait seemed to take hours, even though Cole knew it was just seconds. Anxiously, she shifted from heels to toes. Part of her hoped that nobody was home, but then the locks clicked and the door opened an inch.

Stiffly, she held the six pack up. "Beer?"

The door opened, the porch light turned on, and Adrian Holloway appeared. "I don't drink."

"Neither do I. Mind if I come in?"

Those eyes, depthless little beads in lost white puddles, regarded her. "Sure," he said.

Cole followed him into the kitchen. She put the beers on the table, and Adrian took one and opened it. He raised the can to his mouth and downed it, his Adam's apple bobbing with each gulp, and when he took the can from his lips, he crushed it

73

and pitched it over his shoulder. It landed on the floor with a hollow aluminum clatter.

Cole took a beer for herself. "Adrian, I want to talk to you."

"You were the one who found my sister?"

Cole cracked the beer open. "Yeah. Well, no. It was Craig Campbell, the paper guy. He found her and then called me."

Adrian nodded. He grabbed another beer and took a pull from it. "I had to take my mother to Hampstead a few hours ago. The mental hospital."

It all came out now. Adrian sat at the table and began sobbing into his arms.

It shredded Cole's heart to see a grown man like this. People are divorced from tragedy. On the news, there were always stories about drone strikes, kidnappings, terrorists and shootings. You may hear about it and have an emotional reaction to it, but then you go about your day as if nothing happened. You go to work, visit with friends, and you laugh or get frustrated by the day's trivialities. You aren't there to see the repercussions. You don't see the fire, the grief, or the fresh dead and dying. This was the burden that Cole knew she carried.

She set her beer down and wrapped her arms around Adrian, pressing her face against his heaving back. "I'm sorry, Adrian."

The sobbing eased. Adrian lifted his head and Cole got off him. "So much for a silver lining, Cole," he said, wiping his nose with the back of his hand. "So much for that."

Cole sat down across from him. "Adrian, do you know anything about Tarot?"

"What?"

"They're like these cards. They have pictures on them, and they represent all different abstract concepts. They're used in some"—she snapped her finger as she tried to find the appropriate vocabulary—"some kind of, uh…"

Adrian gave her a puzzled look. "Like séances? Are you talking about witchcraft?"

"Not exactly. Well, maybe. I think I might have a lead on something that the Manchester police don't, but I need your help."

"Cole, I'm exhausted. The police have been here all day, questioning me and my mom. I'm sure that's half the reason why I had to send her off to the hospital."

"I won't pressure you with questions too much. I know you've already been bombarded with them."

"Then what are you asking, Cole?"

Cole took out her phone and looked up the Seven of Swords Tarot, then handed it to Adrian. "Does this imagery look familiar to you?"

"I got no idea what this is." He swiped the screen, looking through all the different cards. "All this is gibberish to me, Cole. I don't..."

He trailed off. His finger stopped swiping and he stared at the screen.

"What is it, Adrian?"

"My mom. Ever since Clarissa and Julia went missing, she's been acting weird. I mean, that's normal, given the circumstances, right? But it was out of context weird, you know?"

"I don't follow."

"Well, the first night I stayed here when I got back from Massachusetts, one thing she said to me was like, 'sins of the father' and that it's 'not our decision that these things happen'. Weird stuff like that."

"Sounds weird, sure, but I could see someone who isn't in a good headspace saying that."

"But there's this, Cole."

He handed her the phone. On the screen was the Moon Tarot. A lobster crawled out of a river that separated a dog and a wolf howling at the moon. A face rested within its sphere that expressed a reserved and yet contemplative expression.

"My mom keeps mentioning the moon," he explained. "She was looking at it the night I came home, talking about the lunar phases. Then again yesterday, just before the search began."

"Is your mom into astronomy?"

"Not at all. Ever since my sister and niece went missing though, she keeps remarking on it. Like it's significant."

"Interesting."

"What's the correlation between what happened to my sister and niece and the Tarot you showed me?"

Cole licked her lips, thinking. She returned the phone to her coat, and then laced her fingers together in front of her on the table. "The Tarot I showed you, the Seven of Swords, has some meaning behind it. Upright, it could mean deception or betrayal. Like someone got away with an evil deed. Reversed, it could mean self-deceit or keeping secrets. I won't get into the details about how I made the connection between this Tarot and your family, but I will say that I think whoever is responsible was trying to send a message."

"What kind of message?"

"That whoever this killer is, they're out for revenge."

"Revenge?" Adrian let out an exasperated sigh. He was getting emotional again. "But why? What did my sister, or even my niece, do to anybody? They didn't deserve what happened to them."

Cole reached across the table and took Adrian's hand. It surprised him—not the gesture, but the touch itself. He was taken by just how gentle her grip was. Cole was a no-nonsense and determined cop, and yet her touch made him think of how nurturing she was in ways that most cops weren't.

"I don't know," she told him. "All this is a stretch. I don't even think it's enough to bother the Manchester police about either, but it's a hunch I have. I need you to do me a favor, Adrian. When are you going to visit your mother in the hospital?"

"I have no idea. I want to see her, but I feel like she needs space."

"As soon as you can, talk to her. Ask her about why the moon is so significant. When you do, call me. You still got my number?"

"I do. Are you really sure that you're onto something?"

"I don't know. It could be something, but it could be nothing. I don't think your mom will cooperate with another police officer. That's why I need you to talk to her. When you do, text me." Cole stood, took another beer, and then hooked her thumb on her belt. "I have some work I've got to do. We're going to find the person responsible for this, Adrian. I promise."

Adrian nodded solemnly. "I trust you."

Cole left the kitchen and stepped out of the house. She stood on the front stoop, zipped up her coat and rubbed her arms. It felt like twenty degrees outside. The neighborhood was dimly lit in the night, and it was because the moon was full, glowing against the black curtain of the sky like a spotlight.

*Sure is beautiful,* Cole thought, looking up at it.

It would have been a lot more beautiful had it not recently held negative connotations. Whoever the killer in Leinster was, they shared a relationship with the moon.

# November 4th

# Blood Moon

At the Leinster Public Library, Grace Davenport stood at the reception desk. In one hand she held a book, and in the other, a scanner. Both were trembling so badly that she had to set the book down on the desk and then hold the scanner with both hands for it to scan properly. The normality of the day's routine was troublesome.

"It's not right," Grace suddenly announced.

Susan was working at a nearby cart, writing down the call numbers for damaged and vandalized books. She set her pen down and looked over her shoulder. "What was that, Grace?"

"Don't play dumb with me, Susan. I know you've been thinking about it, too. Clarissa never did anything to anyone. And Julia"—her voice shook. She dropped the scanner and pressed her hands against her chest. "Julia... why would they? It's so horrible. None of this is right."

Susan's mouth went dry. An ugly guilt consumed her. She wanted to tell her employee—a young woman she'd known since she was a small girl—that everything would turn out okay, but that wasn't possible. It was too late for that.

"I don't like leaving Jeremy alone," Grace went on. "I want him with me and Eddie at home."

"He's not alone, Grace. He's with dozens of students and teachers."

"Exactly! Who are they? I don't know anyone at that school. What if it's one of the teachers?"

Susan's heart skipped. This wasn't something she had considered. All sorts of horror stories sprouted up in the news about unassuming teachers doing things to their pupils.

"I don't want to be here," Grace said. "I want to be with my son. I want to be with my husband. I want all of us together where I know it's safe."

"Grace, if you want to take today off to pick Jeremy up and go home, you can. I can hold fort here."

"Could you? I'm sorry. I know it's just you here."

"It's fine, Grace." She checked her watch—a delicate silver one she wore with the case resting against her wrist. "It's just past noon. There's still plenty of time before school gets out. Let me just run into the back room and make a phone call."

Susan circled around the back shelf and stepped out of sight, the heels of her slip-on shoes tapping lightly against the tiled floor as she went. Grace resumed her work. She had regained some control over her disobedient hands and was able to continue scanning books normally. After about ten books, she set the scanner down and listened. The library was silent. The back room wasn't far, and Grace knew that she would have been able to hear her boss if she was on the phone.

"Susan?" she called. "What are you doing back there?"

"The ceremony of innocence is drowned," a woman's voice recited. It wasn't Susan's. "The best lack all conviction, while the worst are full of passionate intensity."

Through the shelves, Grace could see a figure moving.

"Troubles my sight: somewhere in the sands of the desert, a shape with a lion body and the head of a man, a gaze blank and pitiless as the sun. Were vexed to nightmare by a rocking cradle."

"Who is that?" Grace said.

A woman appeared from behind the back shelf. She wore black from head to toe—a dress with long leather gloves and a funeral veil over her face. When she spoke, it was with a peculiar accent. In her hands she read from an old hardcover book. "And what rough beast, its hour come round at last, slouches towards Bethlehem to be born."

The woman clapped the book shut. Grace couldn't see her face behind that veil save for the faint glimmer of a single eye.

"How did you get in here?" Grace said, backing against the desk. "The back door is locked. You're trespassing."

"You're a librarian, so you must be well-read, is that right?" the woman said. "I am well-read myself. Are you familiar with Nathaniel Hawthorne? Hawthorne's ancestor was a witch judge. He sent innocent men and women to their deaths during the trials in Massachusetts, did you know that? All of Hawthorne's work has this theme—characters who themselves are not guilty of anything but have nonetheless inherited the sins of their ancestors. It's appropriate, I think."

Grace raised her hand to the woman, pointed. "You killed them. It was you who kidnapped Clarissa and her daughter, wasn't it?"

Hung from the bend of the woman's arm was an unkempt purse. She unzipped it and slipped her hand into it.

"Stop!" Grace clawed for the desk drawer behind her, sifting through paperclips and pens until she found a letter opener. She wielded it at the woman like a saber. "Stay back! I don't know you!"

"But I know you." The woman took a step forward. "I especially know your husband, Edward Davenport."

"I told you to stay back!" Grace grabbed her phone from her back pocket and unlocked it.

"You don't want to do that." The woman took yet another step forward. "Put that phone down now. Final warning."

"You won't get anywhere near my family!"

Just before Grace dialed 911, the woman took a long stride forward and flung her hand from her purse. Grace went blind and her nostrils and throat began to burn. She let out a hoarse shriek, the phone fell from her hand and she began manically slashing the letter opener around. Whatever the woman had thrown at her, it was dusty and thick, like a strong powder. It stank like soot.

A ticking sound was heard. It grew louder, and the woman emerged from the hazy black cloud. In her hands she held a metronome, its needle rocking left and right. Grace's eyes stung horribly, and yet she was unable to close them. They watched the needle.

"Lift up your foot and bring it down on your phone," the woman said.

Fear and resistance left Grace, and yet her mind understood what was happening. She was no longer in control of her body. The phone had fallen to the floor next to her. Her foot lifted and came down against it. The screen shattered, and she could hear it crumble beneath her heel.

"Tres bien. Now take that letter opener and drive it into your throat."

Like a snake, her arm raised, pointing the letter opener towards her neck. *Oh god no*, she thought. *Please don't, I want to see my child again please don't—*

The blade pierced her throat. Grace fell to the floor, gagging.

"Grind it now. Twist it."

On command, her first twisted and turned, tearing her throat apart. Blood filled her chest and the back of her mouth, choking her. Tears streamed down the sides of her face and dripped to the floor.

The woman stood over her, watching. One gloved hand came up and pressed a finger against her veil to where her mouth was. "Good. Now, cut open your abdominal wall and take out everything inside."

Grace's mind screamed but her body obeyed. The arm struggled, as her body was weakening, but it extracted the letter opener from her neck, and she pulled her shirt up.


The buses lined up. With his fingers laced in the diamonds of the fence that separated the playground from the front parking lot, Jeremy watched the children line up from afar. He watched his friends George and Franklin got on the bus. His heart wept. He missed his friends.

Once the buses began to depart, Jeremy pouted and sat down on a bench nearby, allowing his feet to kick beneath his seat as he took a granola bar from his bag and ate.

By four o' clock, the buses were gone and most of the students were as well. Jeremy got off the bench and looked through the fence again. Mom's van wasn't anywhere to be seen. Jeremy left the playground and wandered the property. The fifth-grade lacrosse team was playing on the field behind the school, and the McLaughlin Middle School marching band was practicing near the bleachers. Mom wasn't anywhere.

The library was down the street. Jeremy was getting anxious. Maybe Mom was busy? Adjusting the straps of his backpack on his shoulders, he walked down Pierce Street.

It didn't look like any lights were on in the library. Yet, Mom's red van was parked there, along with another car. Jeremy scratched the back of his neck, wondering if he should go inside or walk home. Home was a long way, and despite the unexplainable hesitations he felt, he knew Mom should have been inside. Why did he feel this way?

The bell jingled as Jeremy stepped in, and the door cluttered against its frame behind him. The sound of it lingered in echo throughout the small building.

"Mom?"

No answer. Jeremy approached the front desk and stood on his toes, then patted around on the desktop until his hand found the little bell. The bell rang out, and when Jeremy brought his hand back, he noticed blood on the desk.

A moan crept out from behind the desk—somewhere in the back.

"Mom!" Jeremy cried.

The boy rushed around the reception desk, and he slipped and fell into a massive blood puddle on the floor. For several seconds Jeremy remained on his hands and knees, gawking at what he had fallen into. He tried getting his shoes to grip the floor, but they kept slipping.

"Mom! Mom help!" Jeremy screamed. He slid to a dry spot on the floor, got on his feet and backed away from the blood. A knocked over steel cart was nearby, and several books were settled in the red puddle. Their pages were thick with absorbed bodily fluids.

That moan was heard again. Jeremy ran to the back room. Among the cardboard boxes and electrical equipment, Jeremy found Susan Aimes on the floor naked. Her skin was scabbed all over, making her resemble some harlequin infant. Emerging from the irritated skin were tumors that resembled tree bark and moss. A family of mushrooms stood erect on her back like an infestation of polyps. Branches and twigs poked out of her neck and limbs, and flies dropped larvae into the cracks of her scabs.

"Bonjour, petit garçon."

A woman in a black dress appeared behind him. One gloved hand came up and lifted her veil. The last thing Jeremy Davenport saw was the woman's scarred face, and her single white eye glaring down at him.

"There's a little hollow spot where the kidney should be," Ephrem Jessup said. He took his latex gloves off with a snap and pitched them into a trash bin with a big biological symbol on it. "I think it's safe to assume that one of the kidneys you got in the mail a few days ago came from the body on the slab there."

What remained of Clarissa Holloway was on the steel table. The abdominal cavity was opened wide from sternum to pubic area, and it looked like the organs had been sifted around. The head had been lopped off directly at the shoulder line. Deep cuts passed through the chest, ribs, buttocks and lower back.

"Besides the kidney, the heart is missing as well," Jessup went on, washing his hands in the sink. "Other than that, it looks like everything else is there. Somebody was digging around in there though. It's a total mess."

Lou pulled a handkerchief from his coat and pressed it to his mouth. He hadn't been able to gather much information or even see the body the evening before, as the body was still being inspected. Today though, they let him see it for himself, and he preferred that he hadn't.

What could have been the motive behind something as horrible as this? Not just murder, but decapitation and the removal of organs? It was something Lou couldn't wrap his head around—it was like a Jack the Ripper murder or something. Cole had the imagination for it, but not him.

"May I be frank?" Jessup flicked his wrists over the sink of any straggling water. "One of the police officers earlier described the body here as 'ritualistic'. The crucifixion, beheading, missing organs. It's nonsense to me. Organ harvesting sounds more appropriate."

"Did you find any fingerprints or foreign chemicals?"

Jessup dug a big plastic sheet out of a cabinet and, like some macabre housekeeper, flung it over the slab and allowed it to slowly fall over the body. "No prints, and that's a maybe on the chemicals. We won't know until the lab results come back. Could be tomorrow or the day after."

Lou's phone went off. It was Cole. "Wait a sec," he said, then stepped into a corner. "Cole, where the fuck are you?"

"Lou! Get down here quick!"

"What? What's wrong?"

"The library—the fucking library, Lou! It's bad! It's Grace and Susan!"

Police cruisers lined each side of Pierce Street in front of the Leinster Village Public Library. By the time Cole and Lou arrived on the scene, yellow tape was strapped from telephone poles to orange cones, sanctioning off a huge portion of the road. Investigators, in their dress coats, blue latex gloves and disposable cotton shoe covers, clambered in and out of the building. Cops stood around, watching as a collection of biological evidence bags grew on a plastic fold out table near the sidewalk.

The window next to the front door was vandalized. Smeared on the glass in drying blood was written: "NOVEMBER 1947".

Cole parked the Crown Vic behind one of the cruisers. She and Lou got out and slipped under the police tape, then rushed towards the front door.

"You need gloves and shoe covers," the cop standing by the door said.

An investigator handed the constables what they needed, and then they stepped in. The irony stench of blood hit them once they passed the threshold. More investigators were hunched over a big clotting blood pool behind the front desk, and Cole did her best to avoid looking too closely at it. Then she saw what was in the back room.

It looked as if a giant tree had grown in the corner of the room. Roots threaded through the tiled floor, and vines and moss crawled along the walls, windows and onto the ceiling like a cancerous rash. The tree trunk was deformed—shaped almost like a person. A skull emerged from the bark, along with a ribcage. A single pale arm reached out from the trunk, fingers half curled, with moss growths emerging from scabbed cavities. It was only when Cole saw the silver ring on one of the fingers did she realize that she was looking at the remains of Susan Aimes.

On the floor was a snippet of human hair wrapped around a hunk of tree bark. The color of the hair was the same as Susan's.

On the other side of the village, Amy Gillespie sat on her backyard swing. Her right eye was swollen purple and her jaw was aching. The TV could be heard in the house behind her, as well as her mother's loud gossiping over the phone.

Greg Chandler had been at it again that morning. She had crossed paths with him in the hallway while Amy was going to the bathroom. He had shoved her into a locker and licked her face. When she tried to fight back, he had punched her and then shoved her to the floor.

Having missed the bus, Amy walked home, and the moment she went up to the front door she could already hear the TV on inside. Mom was awake, and Amy didn't have the strength to even look at her, so she went around the house and just stayed in the backyard. There, sitting on her swing, she remained.

So badly she wanted Dad to be home. The last thing she wanted was to be in the house alone with Mom right now. All she wanted was to talk to somebody about what happened to her. It was all just awful. Why did everything have to be so unfair?

"It doesn't have to be, chérie."

A voice startled her. Something moved around in the trees at the back of the yard. Amy hopped off the swing and took a step towards the woods. "Hello?" she called.

"What's wrong, Amy?"

"Who are you?"

"You're scared. I'm sorry. I don't mean to alarm you. See…?" The branches rustled. A woman stepped out from the trees and stood with her gloved hands neatly folded in front of herself. A veil covered her face. "My name is Angelique. And you are Amy."

"How do you know my name? What are you doing back there?"

The veil gently blew forward and fell in with each breath and word the woman took and spoke. "I live back here. You found my home a few days ago. I saw you."

Amy's eyes widened. "That place with the old staircase and fireplace. And that creepy cellar. That was…?"

"My home. Or what remains of it. I know your name because I can hear your mother shouting sometimes. I can hear her abuse you and your father."

It was discomforting to hear this. What went on in Amy's home was private and emotional. To know that a stranger had listened in on this was intrusive, but it was also alleviating. Somehow, someone knowing about her situation was comforting.

"Amy," the woman took a step forward, "I know how lonely you are. I see you often in this backyard. You haven't even anyone to push you while on your swing."

"My Mom drinks," Amy said quietly, as if she were ashamed herself to even admit it. "And my Dad loves her. He loves me too, and he wants to help us, but mom hurts him. And she hurts me."

"You poor girl. I'm so sorry you have to live like this."

"I would do anything to escape." Amy hadn't intended to confess this, but it came out. "My house isn't home."

The woman nodded. "Would you like to see something?"

"What?"

Angelique held her hand out to the swing. "Take a seat."

Amy she sat on it.

"Hang on tightly."

Something gently pushed her forward, and then pulled her back. It began weakly, like a breeze, but each time she went forward, a warm force moved her a little stronger.

The woman stood to the side with her arm out, fingers extended. When she moved it left, that force behind Amy was felt, and she was pushed forward. When she moved it right, Amy was pushed back.

"Wow!" Amy cheered.

"Hold tightly."

It got to the point where she could see her feet touch the horizon. Amy started laughing, and the woman laughed with her. Outwardly, the woman appeared strange, even threatening. And yet, her laugh was intimate. It was a reassuring, youthful laugh, gentle and girly. Excitement filled Amy's chest as the wind flew through her hair.

The swing slowed, coming to a crawling halt. Amy hopped off. "That was amazing, lady. How did you do that?"

"Magic. I can do all sorts of things."

"Really?"

"Yes." The woman's voice went low and serious, and she knelt to be eye level with the girl. "You know, I can understand your pain, petite fille. I too came from a house that didn't feel like home."

Amy looked at the ground and began picking at her fingers.

"Look at me, enfant."

Through that veil, Amy could see an eye. "Yes?"

"My parents mistreated me because I could do things like what I just showed you. Magic. They were frightened of me. So, I ran away. I come from a place far from here, another country to the north."

"Is that why you talk funny?"

The woman laughed. "You could say! But your mother, she only abuses you because she is afraid of you."

"Why is she afraid?"

"Because"—the woman reached out, held the girl by the chin—"she knows that you deserve a better mother than her. Let me ask you, enfant, do you want a new home?"

Amy nodded. "Yes. A new home for my Dad too."

"I think I can provide that."

"You can?"

"Yes. I have another magic trick to show you. Would you like to see?"

Amy smiled—a tender expression despite missing one of her front teeth. "Yes. What is it?"

The woman lifted her arm, where a little purse hung from the bend of her elbow. She unzipped it. "I have a magical potion. I want you to take a deep breath, my child."

"Hey!"

Standing at the back door of the house was Amy's mom, Frances Gillespie. Her nose and cheeks were bright red and her flannel was misbuttoned. A mixed expression of terror and rage swam across her face, and she stumbled down the back steps— tripping once, then regaining her balance—and charged across the yard to the woman.

"Who are you?" Frances grabbed Amy by the hair and yanked her away. "Get the fuck away from my child!"

"Ow! Mom! Let go!"

"Shut up, Amy. What did I tell you about talking to people I don't know?" She twisted her daughter's hair, ignored her cries, then shot a fierce drunken scowl at the woman. "Who are you? You have about ten seconds to explain yourself before I call the constable."

The woman crossed her arms. The single visible eye behind her veil seemed to scan Frances.

For a moment, France's rage simmered, and a flicker of intimidation flew through her, but then the rage returned. "I asked you a question, lady!"

"If I recall, it was your grandfather who started the fire," the woman said. "Yes, I remember now. Same lips, same eyes, same nose. You and he look remarkably alike."

"What the fuck are you talking about?"

"Is your grandfather, Arthur, still alive, Frances Thatch?"

Frances blinked. How did this woman know her maiden name and her grandfather? Grandpa Arthur died when she was eleven years old. "You—what?" she stammered. "I'm calling the constable!"

"Wait!" The woman threw her hand up. Her tone became submissive. "Please, don't call the constable."

"And why the fuck shouldn't I?"

"Because I can pay you."

Frances blinked. Her tone changed. "Pay me, huh."

Amy reached up and grabbed her mother's hand, which still gripped her hair. "Mom, please let go of me. It hurts."

"Shut up, Amy. I'm taking care of this." She refocused her gaze on the veiled woman. "How much are we talking about here?"

"Well," the woman slipped her hand into the little purse. "Let me just see what I have in here…"

Cole pulled up to the constable office and parked it. A flock of ravens had settled on the power lines above, cawing and cooing. She eyed them strangely. The birds seemed to sense that she noticed them, and they flew away out of sight.

"Lou, what the fuck is happening?" she said.

"I don't know." Lou thumbed some tobacco under his lip. "I don't know what I saw today."

"That was Susan, Lou. Something happened to her. I've never seen tumors like that. It's like she was turned into something. I saw her ring."

"It looked like she'd been turned into a fuckin tree or some shit."

"Someone is terrorizing the village, Lou. They're deliberately targeting people, then making a big display of it. It's been an escalation—theatrical, almost. First, a missing child and their mother. Then, the display on their front lawn. And now this, with another mother and her child missing, with blood everywhere and a message on the window. It's a showcase. But how are the Holloways and the Davenports connected?"

"Cole!" Lou pointed. "Look, across the square."

The lights of the municipal building were on, and about three dozen people were gathered in front of it—many Cole recognized from the search parties. Near the entrance was Eddie

Davenport. The front of his shirt was wet from sweat, and his hair was a wild mess over his glasses. The thickness of the lenses made his bugged-out eyes look even more frenetic.

"Shit, that's Eddie," Lou said. "I thought the police took him to the station in Manchester."

"We'd better check on him."

They got out and crossed the square. Eddie saw them and rushed to them. "Cole! Lou! It's good that you're here."

"Eddie, we know what happened," Lou began. "We need you to just keep cool. Understand?"

"Keep cool?" His glasses nearly fell off, and he pushed them back up his nose. "My wife and son are missing, Deputy Wolfe, and you want me to keep cool?"

Tactfulness was never one of Lou's stronger personality traits, Cole knew, so she pulled him back by the sleeve and stepped forward. "Are you organizing another town meeting, Eddie?"

"Yes. This is no longer an isolated incident, Cole. Everyone is threatened now. This involves the entire village." He pressed his thumb to his chest. "This involves *me* now!"

"Eddie, we can't—"

"Don't tell me what I can and can't do, Colquitt! I will not let Grace turn out the way Clarissa did. I won't let anything happen to my little boy! As selectman, I need you in this meeting! Mickey Collins will be here soon. We're putting together another search party."

"Eddie, we've already tried that!"

"Then what am I supposed to do? Just let this crazy bastard kill my"—he stopped, unable to finish the sentence. "I'm finding my wife and child, Cole. Now, get in here and help us!"

Eddie went in, leaving the door open for the constables.

Lou shrugged. "What can we do, Cole? Wiggle our dicks around?"

"Speak for yourself, Lou."

Lou stepped in. Just as Cole turned to follow him, she stopped herself. A raven had perched itself on the back of a wooden bench nearby. It watched her inquisitively, tilting its head to the side.

"Little shit," Cole muttered. She grabbed a rock from the curb and pitched it at the bird. The raven yapped and flew away.


Hampstead Hospital, at a distance, could easily be mistaken for some sort of old-fashioned courthouse. It was a modest, nondescript building with a triangular pavilion and white pillars out front. The only indication that it was a psychiatric hospital was a red sign near the street that read: HAMPSTEAD HOSPITAL – NO EMERGENCY SERVICES".

Adrian parked in the visitor lot and stepped inside.

The lobby was plain, like an office building. It had a gray carpet with white walls, framed photos of old men in glasses, and a big grandfather clock ticking away near a coffee table with health magazines on it. The façade of banal normality was broken only by the shouts and cries emitting through the walls.

"May I help you?" a young woman in a gray suit at the front desk asked.

"I'm visiting my mother. Martha Holloway."

A woman in scrubs stepped in and summoned him. She walked him through the hospital to a wooden door with a sign on it that simply read "19".

It was a small room, with a single bed next to a sofa and a table. There was little else. No paintings, plants or anything else. It was like a sterile motel room. Martha sat in a chair in front of the window, watching the world outside slowly go dark with the coming night.

"Mom." Adrian sat down on the arm of the sofa next to her. "What are you looking at?"

"The moon. Look at it now."

Adrian leaned and peeked out the window. There was still daylight, but it was waning. The moon was full, but it was not white anymore. It was dark red. There were clouds in the sky, as if it were going to rain or snow soon, and the illumination of the moon bled crimson against them.

"This is the final phase," Martha said.

Adrian examined her face. Something wasn't right. The sluggish nature of her movements, the dilation in her pupils, and the color of her skin all indicated that she was on heavy drugs.

"Mom, I need you to help me. What is so significant about the moon?"

"How are things in Leinster, Adrian?"

"They're bad, Mom. Real bad."

"You know, I've been thinking a lot about our family, Adrian. Want to know one of my favorite memories of you and your sister? When you were a baby, not long before your dad left, our bathtub wasn't working properly. I put you down in the kitchen sink and bathed you there. Your sister, she wanted to help clean you up, so she got up on a chair and snatched the soap out of my hand. She washed what little hair there was on your head. Even when you were a baby, she had such affection for you."

The anecdote made Adrian's throat constrict, but he kept his composure. "Mom, I need you to tell me about the moon. It's clear that there's a connection between what's happening to Leinster and the moon. Tell me what it is."

"There was this other time, too. Clarissa was home from school, and you came home before I did, and—"

"Mom!"

Those drugged eyes searched for him. "Adrian, your temper."

"Leinster is in trouble, Mom. The constable, Kaysen, might have a hunch on something that could save lives."

"What lives can be saved? My daughter and granddaughter are gone. I couldn't help them."

"That's my sister and niece you're talking about, so don't give me that crap. If you don't help me, then more mothers will lose their children. Do you understand?"

"Are the Davenports in trouble? Grace, Jeremy and Eddie?"

"Yes, they are. Not long before I left to come here, I heard that the library got attacked."

"I knew it. I knew it would happen. Frances Thatch... she must be next. Isn't she married now?"

"What did you mean by 'sins of the father', Mom?"

"Adrian, I can't."

"Yes, you can! You know something, and you need to tell me before it's too late!"

A tear rolled down her face, and she placed a hand against her son's unshaven face. She contemplated him with dozy, inebriated eyes. "At first, I suspected, but I discarded the idea. Truth be told, it's always been in the back of my mind, but I wasn't sure if I should believe it or not. Now though, with the moon appearing as it is, my daughter and granddaughter gone, and with you telling me about the Davenports, I know it must be true. Leinster is doomed. Four families brought its end. With their blood—with *our* blood—the village will burn."

"You need to stop being vague."

"Your grandfather was such a tormented man. You know how he always used to drink, how he treated me growing up. It was because he carried something with him that he knew would affect me and my children. When I was young, and he drank, sometimes he'd tell me what he did that damned our family. I never believed him when I was growing up, but I always wondered. Now, I know it's true."

"What did he say?"

Martha pulled him close, pressed her lips to his ear: "Davenport. Thatch. Graven. Holloway."

She told him everything.


It was getting late and Ephrem Jessup was the last one at the coroner's office. With the key ring twirling around his finger, he went around locking every door and shutting off the lights. There wasn't a lot he had planned for the night. Ever since the body of the Holloway woman turned up, he'd been on the phone or talking to the police nonstop. He was tired.

As he went to the stairs leading to the back exit, he put his hand on the light switch, but stopped himself short of flipping it.

The door to the morgue was opened and the light within crept out into the corridor. Strange. The morgue was always the first place he locked up.

One of the freezer doors was open. A ripped-up leather bag was on the floor in front of it. A pinkish clear fluid—a mixture of blood and formaldehyde—was puddled all over the place. Brownish footsteps lead from the body bag to the door. Despite locking it, the morgue door could still be opened from the inside.

The name card on the opened freezer door read: "HOLLOWAY, CLARISSA MARIE".

Blissfully ignorant of the entire day's events, having pushed overtime at the shop with little time to rest, Samuel Gillespie pulled up the narrow driveway of his mobile home. The lights were off in the house, but the glow of the TV could be seen through the windows. That meant Frances was asleep. If the lights were on, that meant she was awake, but if the lights were off and the TV was on, that usually meant she was passed out on the recliner. Maybe he could spend a little time with Amy without having to deal with her.

Quietly, as not to wake his wife, Samuel shut the car door and slipped into the house. The recliner was empty. Not thinking much of this, Samuel shut the TV off, went down the hallway and knocked on his daughter's bedroom door. "Amy? Are you home?"

When no one answered, he poked his head in. Nobody was there.

"Amy? Where are you?"

Silence. Samuel began to panic. The situation with the Holloways flashed through his mind, and then he remembered how his daughter had wandered into the woods the other day. He grabbed a flashlight from the equipment cupboard in the kitchen and slapped the porch light on. Through the mesh of the screen door, he could see the blood. He rushed outside.

The blood coated the dirt and grass beneath the tree swing, which rocked gently in the autumn breeze. The torn up remains of his wife's blouse lay nearby. Samuel gripped it in his fist. "Frances! Amy!" he shouted at the trees.

Turning on the flashlight, he entered the woods.

Through the bare branches above, the moon glowed bright red. It was something Samuel hadn't noticed until now, and it did no favors for his state of mind. The beam of his flashlight cut through the darkness, and all he could see were tree trunks. They seemed to enclose around him the further he went into the woods.

"Frances! Amy! Please say something!"

A branch to his left snapped, followed by leaves crunching. Samuel froze. Part of him wanted to shine his light on whatever it was, thinking that it may be his wife or child. Another part of him didn't want to. Those leaves crunched again, approaching him. Samuel began walking in the opposite direction. As he picked up the pace, so did whatever was following him. He began to run. Violent footfalls were hot on his trail.

"Help!" he shouted. "Somebody! Any—"

Something hit him across the face. The flashlight dropped from his hand, his feet flew out from beneath him and he fell in the mud. Stars filled his eyes and he could feel the warm sensation of blood on his mouth. Judging by the bark around his chin and cheek, he ran headfirst into a low tree branch. His hands searched for the flashlight. The beam could be seen nearby, pointing against a mossy rock. He grabbed it and pointed the light ahead and saw three naked headless bodies standing in front of him.

One looked to have been dead for days, while the other two were fresh. All were disemboweled and decapitated at the shoulders. They resembled forest nymphs, covered in all sorts of paints and flowers. One pressed its hand against a tree and took a step forward. Judging by the body shape and the mole on the ribs beneath the left breast, Samuel knew that he was staring at the headless corpse of his wife.

Samuel screamed, and he got up and turned to run. A veiled woman in black stood behind him. Her arm shot out, grabbed him by the hair and yanked him forward. He dropped the flashlight and he tried grabbing the woman's hand to pry it off, but her grip was savage. Scissors clipped and snipped, and he was let go. Samuel snatched the flashlight off the ground and pointed it at the woman.

"Un cochon," she said. In one hand she held a clump of Samuel's hair. In the other she wielded a pair of scissors. She put the scissors away into a small purse on her arm, then took what looked like an animal hoof from it and wielded it and the hair clump before her. The light glowed through her veil, and Samuel could see the woman's ruined face. She was grinning.

"Vous deviendrez un cochon," she said.

Samuel fled. Her voice whispered in his ears as he went. It propelled him to go faster and without looking back.


Eddie Davenport and Mickey Collins sat in their chairs on the stage of the old theater-turned-town hall. To their left Cole and Lou were seated. In the theater chairs before the stage were over three dozen concerned townsfolk.

Eddie was anxious. His foot tapped against the stage floor in fast raps. "The situation here in Leinster has gone from bad to worse," he said. "What began as a kidnapping has spiraled into an attack on our community. There is a predator somewhere here in the village."

"We're still waiting on what the Manchester Police Department has to say," Mickey said. "According to Chief McQuarrie, we should be getting a press conference tomorrow morning, but time is of the essence, so some answers now would be nice. Cole, where do you and Lou stand with the police?"

Cole threw her hands up. "It's out of our goddamned hands now, Mickey. They've kept us in the dark as much as you. Lou and I are granted only a certain amount of authority here in the village. It's still Manchester's turf."

"It could be anyone!" a man in a trucker cap shouted. "The killer could be in this room with us right now, listening to everything we say!"

"We can't jump to any conclusions like that," Mickey said. "We need to get a grip on ourselves and think."

"There has to be another search party," Eddie interjected. "We need to split up and cover as much ground as possible."

"We already tried that!" a woman called. "We didn't find anything. It's a waste of time."

"God damn it, it is *not* a waste of time! This is my family, do you understand? My wife—my *child!*"

Mickey put his hand on Eddie's arm. "You have got to calm down, Ed."

"Don't tell me to calm down! Jeremy is out there with some psycho, and you want me to be diplomatic about it? I want people out there looking for him now!"

"This is getting us nowhere," another man in the audience said. "The Manchester police must know something we don't. Cole, you used to be a cop in Manchester. Don't you know anyone you can talk to? Get some insider info?"

The room went afoul with arguments and riffraff. Eddie fanned the flames while Mickey tried to talk him down. Everyone was shouting over one another. Lou rubbed his temples and shook his head. Cole hid her face in her hair.

"How could this shit get any worse, Cole?" Lou said.

A voice shouted from behind the stage curtain: "I would like to say a word!"

The room hushed. Heavy thumps sounded against the stage floor, the curtain parted, and a woman emerged from backstage. From head to toe she wore all black, and a veil covered her face. By her side, she held an old wool knapsack.

Eddie stood. "Who are you?"

The woman observed the audience. "It is good to see so many of Leinster's villagefolk gathered here. I wanted to see many of you."

"I asked you a question," Eddie growled.

"My name is Angelique de Lapointe. I have watched this village grow and change for decades. I remember when they converted this old theater into the town hall. I watched the old tanneries undergo renovations and become homes. I remember when Jointer Avenue, Eaglewood Street and Renault Street were still dirt roads. The village trapper, Yosemite Greenman, used to cart his wagon into town from Renault Street. I remember him."

Everyone looked at each other. Everything she talked about were things many couldn't remember personally, but had heard from their parents or grandparents.

"And you, mademoiselle." She pointed at Cole. "You've only been constable here for a few years. You replaced Jasper Graven. You've seen so much here in Leinster Village over the past few days. I'm sure you wish you could have had it easy here after you shot that addict. Raymond Sears was his name, is that right?"

A bead of sweat rolled down Cole's temple. "Excuse me?"

"Yes, it was Raymond. You paralyzed him, and he killed himself. You wanted to run away from this, yes?"

Eddie stepped towards her. "You're responsible, aren't you? You're the one who has been terrorizing us."

"I may have some answers for you, monsieur."

"Then answer me this, lady. Where is my wife?" He stammered his words and swallowed. "Where is my son?"

"You want to know where your family is, yes?"

"Stop playing games and tell me!"

"I have your wife with me."

"Where is she? Tell me where she is right now!"

"Your wife is right here, monsieur. I will fetch her."

Angelique lifted the knapsack, pulled the string on it and reached inside. Like a rabbit trick, she pulled Grace Davenport's gray head out of the sack by the hair. The eyes were purple and the bottom lip sagged.

Nobody in the room moved or spoke. They just stared at the head. Angelique held it for Cole and Lou to see, then held it to the audience, and then turned it to Eddie and Mickey

The eyes opened. One eye looked at Eddie and the other lazily considered the floor. Its tongue flapped around, and the wheezing sound of air passing through its severed throat was heard.

"Eddie?" it croaked.

Eddie's face went white. "Grace?"

"Eddie, is that you? What's happening to me? I'm scared—I can't see anything. It's so cold. Where's our son?"

Eddie grabbed his hair and began tearing thick tufts out of his scalp. "Make it *STOP!*"

"I have Clarissa Holloway in here, too," Angelique said, jiggling the knapsack. "Would you like to see her as well? Perhaps Frances Thatch?"

Eddie collapsed to the floor. Mickey gasped, flew from his chair and started shaking him.

"That's enough!" Lou took his gun from its holster and aimed it at the woman. "Put it away! Set the sack on the floor and put your damn hands up!"

Angelique returned the head into the sack, set it on the floor, and then put her hands in the air.

"I'm gonna enjoy this, you piece of shit." Lou kept his gun on her as he marched across the stage. He grabbed her wrist and went to put it behind her back, but in one swift motion, Angelique turned, lifted her veil, and spat a stinking black fluid into Lou's face.

Lou shrieked, dropped his gun and clawed at his face. Angelique drew a pair of scissors from the front of her dress, grabbed him by the hair and messily snipped off a clump of it. Lou lost his balance and fell onto the floor.

"Cole!" he shouted. "The fuckin bitch spat this burning shit all over my goddamn face!"

The constable rushed to him, took several tissues from her coat and started wiping his face. Whatever it was that Angelique spat on him, it was irritating his skin bad enough to turn it red. It stank like roadkill, too.

Cole looked up at the woman. An ugly yellow grin formed behind her veil. She held up the patch Lou's hair. It dripped with blood—she must have nicked his scalp when she cut it.

"Un oiseau," she said. "Vous deviendrez un oiseau."

The audience scattered. A few scrambled over the seats and ran into each other. They cluttered towards the back of the room where the exits were. People shouted, cried, and yelled at each other to move out of the way.

"She's the killer!" somebody cried. "Somebody stop her!"

Angelique returned the scissors to the front of her dress, along with Lou's hair, and then produced a small vial from her glove. She held it up and popped the cap off with her thumb.

"1947!" she exclaimed. "This is for 1947!"

She drank it and smashed the empty vial to the floor. She gurgled, lifted her veil, and a stream of glowing orange fire erupted from her face. Like a fire breathing performer, she circled the room with a stream of embers flowing from her mouth. The curtains quickly blazed, as did the ceiling. It spread fast, crawling along the walls and consuming the theater seats. The audience screamed and stumbled over one another as they tried to escape.

"Lou!" Cole pulled him up from under his arms. "I need you to get up!"

"My fuckin eyes are burning, Cole."

"Get up! Now!"

"Fuck, what is happening?"

"Just hold on!"

Cole dragged Lou over to a window and she smashed her elbow through it. The woman in black cackled as the roaring fire consumed the building. Her laughter boomed over the chaos and the shrill cries of people burning alive.

"1947!" she kept shouting. "1947!"

Lou managed to get his arm over the windowsill, and Cole lifted his legs so that he went up and through the window. Once he was outside, she pulled herself out after him.

Merrimack Square was filled with people. Some were on the sidewalk, others stood beside their idling cars. Many were on their cell phones or taking photos. They gazed at the inferno in the middle of their village.

Cole dragged Lou over to the Crown Vic, opened the passenger door and set him down in the seat. He was grunting and cursing, rubbing his reddening face. Blood from his scalp ran down his forehead.

Cole took the radio microphone off the dashboard and shouted into it: "This is Colquitt Kaysen, constable of Leinster

Village. We need the fire department on Merrimack Square right now! The town hall is burning down and there are people still inside!"

"We already have units dispatched to Leinster Village, Constable Kaysen," the dispatcher reported. "We're receiving over a dozen phone calls about it now."

Sirens bellowed through the night, along with the loud horn of a fire truck. They echoed through the streets, and at some points, Samuel even saw their lights.

Samuel had locked himself in the bathroom and spent the better part of an hour sitting on the toilet, clutching a kitchen knife to his chest. His mind held no rational thoughts, his heart no emotion other than terror. What he had seen in the woods behind his house kept flashing through his mind. The three headless corpses, standing and moving, looking at him without eyes. He kept seeing his wife's mole beneath her breast, and the opening between her ribs and naval where her intestines leaked. The clean cut at her shoulders where her head should have been haunted him. Then there was the woman in black, holding a clump of his hair.

Part of him wanted to call the police. Another part reminded him that in order to do that, he'd need to unlock the bathroom door and leave, and he wasn't about to do that just yet. Anywhere in the house, those three headless bodies could be wandering about, looking for him. The only room he knew was safe was the bathroom, where there wasn't even a window. Where had he even left his cell phone? Had it fallen out while he was in the woods? When he checked his pockets, he couldn't feel it anywhere.

"Amy," he whimpered. "I'm sorry."

A pain surged through his wrist, sharp enough to pull him out of his grief. Pressure emerged within the tendons of his hand. Samuel dropped the knife. "Ack!" he cried, gripping his knuckles. All over, his body burned like fire. The air left his lungs and he fell off the toilet onto his hands and knees, gagging.

Something was coming out of his hand, between the knuckles. It pushed against the skin and spread his fingers apart. The pain was abhorrent, and Samuel glared at his hand as something sprouted its way out between his fingers like some insect. The skin ripped and blood dripped to the tiled floor.

"Oh god," he gasped. "What's happening to me?"

All at once he remembered the woman in black. She had snipped some of his hair off and said something to him—what had she done to him?

A large bone of keratin grew from his hand.

Pressure built up behind his face. Samuel clawed at his eyes, trying to scream, but was unable to. All that came out were squeals. Something was coming out of the middle of his face, rupturing his nose and pushing his eyes away. Blood filled his throat. When he looked down at his deformed hand, he saw a pink hoof bulging out of it. Soon after, his legs began to contort and twist.

Merrimack Square was filled with blue flashing lights, dancing orange flames and pillowing smoke. Two firetrucks and an ambulance were parked in the square, along with three police cruisers. Two firefighters sprayed out the last of the embers while more navigated the splintered black ruins of what had once been the Leinster municipal building. EMTs stepped out of the rubble with big rubber boots and masks, carting body bags between them to the ambulance. There were already eight confirmed deaths, with seven injuries—three of whom were in critical condition and would soon be airlifted to Boston.

Among the dead was Edward Davenport. Cole recognized him when he was pulled from the wreckage. The only part of him that she could recognize was the bright blue button up shirt that he had been wearing.

The constables sat on the hood of their Crown Vic in a daze. None of it seemed real. Yet, they had seen it all happen. Lou was patting his face with a rag given to him by one of the

EMTs, and his skin was burned and scarred like he'd just gotten over a bad case of chickenpox.

"It's snowing."

Cole looked at Lou. "Huh?"

Lou pointed. "I said it's snowing."

Little white specks fell from the sky. Cole held her hand out and a snowflake landed in her palm. It melted against her skin. It built up on the pavement around the body bags, on the vehicles, and on the wooden benches.

"Cole!"

Adrian Holloway was jogging towards them, looking aghast at the destruction. "Holy shit, Cole. What happened here?"

"Adrian, this woman—she was like a fucking demon or something," Cole said, getting off the Crown Vic. "She had Grace—her god damned head! And there was fire, and—"

"She spat this fuckin black shit all over my face," Lou growled. He raised his face up and poured water from a plastic bottle into his eyes.

"It's pandemonium! It was a woman in a veil, like she was dressed for a funeral."

"I know. It's true." Adrian said.

"What's true?"

"Where the fuck have you been, kid?" Lou shook his head to clear his face of any lingering water.

"I was talking to my mom, at the hospital." Adrian looked at the remains of the municipal building. A ninth body bag was added to the growing row near the ambulance. "Do you mind if we talk about it somewhere else?"

At Martha Holloway's house, Cole and Lou sat at the kitchen table. The lamp above shadowed the edges of the room. The coffee maker gurgled, and Adrian emerged from the dark and placed two mugs in front of the constables.

"So," Lou said, stirring the coffee with the tip of his pinky. "You got an explanation for the crazy shit Cole and I just saw?"

"I might." Adrian sat across from them. "It makes sense, but some of it might also be unreliable. My mother isn't in the best place mentally, and she's under the influence of a lot of drugs."

"So, what you're telling us is that we need to take all this with a pinch of salt." Lou flippantly slung his arm around the back of his chair.

"If you've got any other explanation, then I'm open to hear it, Lou," Adrian said.

"At this point, if you told me that space aliens were attacking, I'd probably believe it," Cole said.

Adrian laced his fingers together on the table. "My mother told me a lot of things today. It adds up. It has something to do with my grandfather. I never met my grandfather, because he died when I was about five years old. Cirrhosis. He drank a lot. Sometimes, he'd start wallowing in self-pity. Lock himself up in the attic and just talk to himself. Once, when my mother was around twelve, she went up there while he was alone drinking. He told her a story about something he did when he was younger. She never brought it up to him again afterwards, and she wasn't even sure if he remembered telling her the story when he sobered up afterwards.

"Once, there was this guy who lived in Leinster—his name was Peter Bell. Bell ran an antique shop here in town, and he was a war hero, too. He fought the Japanese in the Solomon Islands from 1943 until their surrender, and he came back with a Silver Star and Purple Heart. A lot of people knew him around the village."

"Bell," Cole repeated. "Lou, wasn't Bell the name of that grave that was desecrated in the Eternal Light Cemetery?"

"Shit, I think you're right, Cole."

"Desecrated?" Adrian repeated. "What do you mean?"

"A grave was robbed a few days ago, not long after your niece and sister went missing," Cole said. "It belonged to Peter Bell. It was all dug up and the remains were stolen."

"That makes sense. That just makes everything more valid."

"What do you mean?"

"Let me finish. A year after the war, a woman came to the village. She didn't have any money, wore ratty clothes, and didn't even speak English. The most anyone knew about her was that she was from Canada, and had been working at a mill in Manchester where a bunch of French Canadians got laid off.

"Over in Merrimack Square, she put out a hat to collect money and performed magic tricks for people. She'd make birds appear in her hands, do card tricks, and turn people's shirts from blue to brown, then back to blue again. Things like that. The constable at the time, Jerimiah Graven—Jasper's father—he didn't take to the woman's vagrancy or panhandling, so he arrested her. A day before she was to be transferred to the state police barracks in Bedford, she got released on bail. You want to take a guess at who bailed her out?"

"It was Peter Bell, wasn't it?" Cole said.

"Exactly. Peter knew the woman a little, because his antique shop was right on the square. The woman had once charmed him by making a rose appear out of thin air in his lapel. I guess he took a liking to her, so when he'd heard Jerimiah had taken her in, he bailed her out.

"Peter lived over on Farmstead Road. They closed the road after a flood in the fifties, and the woods grew around it. Peter helped the woman get back on her feet and even taught her some English. Her name was Angelique de Lapointe."

Lou slapped his hand on the table. "That bitch! That's exactly what she said her name was!"

"Peter had Angelique work at the antique shop with him. A lot of the townsfolk didn't trust her. They knew she had been a vagrant. At the time, immigrants weren't welcome around here. A lot of people were displaced due to the war. French, Italian, Russian—there was intense animosity towards them around Manchester. Angelique wasn't from France—she was Canadian—but it was close enough and people didn't know the difference.

"The kids though, they liked her, and they visited her at the shop a lot. I guess it meant a lot to her. Besides Peter, she didn't have anyone else. The kids would talk about the magic she would do, and the adults only seemed to resent her more for it. They thought she had some sort of influence over their kids."

"It sounds like she and Peter were close," Lou said.

"They were engaged. They were supposed to get married around Christmas of 1947. It never came to pass."

"Why?"

"They were murdered. In October of that year, one of the kids Angelique was friends with got hit by a car in the square. It happened just as she was closing the antique shop. A bunch of people gathered around the boy, and Angelique pushed herself through the crowd and saw him. The kid was only about eleven years old.

"She dropped her things and lifted his shirt. The edge of the car bumper or something had cut his abdomen open. Angelique took some kind of vial from her coat and poured it all over the wound, then pressed her hand against it. She chanted something, and slowly the bleeding stopped. When she took her hand away, the gash in the kid's stomach was gone.

"Everyone backed away as she and the kid got up. There was a lot of relief, but confusion as well. Everyone had seen how close the boy was to death, but Angelique's intervention with no medical expertise had revived him. Well, word got around. With all the magic tricks, and now this miracle act…"

"People suspected her?" Cole said.

"Of witchcraft. A few weeks after that afternoon, a group of people conspired at the town hall—the very town hall that burned to the ground this evening. They agreed to have four people drive out to Peter's house on Farmstead Road late in the night. They lit several Molotov cocktails and threw them through the windows. The house burned all night, and Angelique and Peter never stepped out. Peter was buried in the Eternal Light Cemetery, but nobody knew what happened to Angelique's remains. The ruins of the house were left as they were, and the property was never purchased again."

"Who were the four people responsible?"

"Arthur Thatch, James Davenport, Jerimiah Graven, and my grandfather, Richard Holloway."

"Jesus," Lou said.

"Who's Arthur Thatch?" Cole asked.

"That must have been Frances Gillespie's grandfather," Lou said. "Thatch is her maiden name—she married that poor sucker Samuel Gillespie who works fixing cars."

"Then James Davenport must be Eddie's grandfather."

"Jerimiah was Jasper's dad."

Adrian went on: "This veiled woman, Angelique de Lapointe. She was a witch who was murdered along with her fiancé in 1947, by four people under conspiracy of the village."

"Now, she's back somehow," Cole said. "And she's hunting down the ancestors of those four people. Jasper is already dead and so are his two sons. She got your sister and niece, and she also got Grace Davenport and her son, and"—she paused—"she got Eddie, too. In the fire."

Lou stood. "Samuel, Frances, and their little girl, Amy."

"She's going to get them next!" Cole got up and took her keys from her pocket. "We have to help them now!"

"Adrian, you need to come with us, understand? We can't leave you alone with this crazy lady. Cole and I have to help the Gillespies right now, so grab…"

Lou trailed off. His face blushed, and then went white. He stumbled, pressed a hand against his forehead and held on to the back of a chair for balance. "Whoa," he said.

"You all right, Lou?" Cole said.

"I don't know. I just got dizzy and nauseous. Something feels off. Something—shit!" Lou grimaced and pressed his arms against his abdomen. "My whole damn body is going hot."

"I got the aspirin in the cruiser, Lou. Lets—"

He knocked Cole back and let out an excruciated cry. Something was poking out of his face, just above his nose, beneath the skin.

"Cole, Adrian—what's—" were his last words.

A beak emerged from his face, splitting it apart. His screams became gargled, and he fell to the floor. The back of his coat pressed outwards, ripping it. Blood poured from underneath his clothes. Some sort of arm broke through the back of his coat, splattering more blood against the wall. Another arm broke through. Both were covered in black feathers, and they stretched themselves out, knocking over a chair and a glass on the table. They were long bird wings, unfolding like two massive oriental hand fans. Lou's garbled voice became shrill squawks, and he lifted a hand up to Cole for help. Talons tore through his palm and knuckles.

Adrian grabbed Cole by her coat and dragged her out. The bird man screeched, and it got up and flailed after them. Feathers flew and framed photos fell off the walls, shattering against the floor. Adrian threw Cole through the front door, leapt out himself, and then slammed the door shut behind them. Talons scraped against the wooden door as it rattled in its frame.

"What's—what—" Cole stuttered. Her eyes bulged, staring at the door as it shook and bent from the animal-man behind it.

"Cole! Get in the car!"

They fled to the Crown Vic. Cole started the vehicle up and they tore out of the driveway and sped down Sanders Street.

The blood moon dominated the sky. Everything near its vicinity seemed to become tainted by it: the clouds, the stars, the night itself. Adrian stood in a field of tall grass, staring at it.

Cole was a few yards away, kneeling by the Merrimack River. Her hand was in the water, feeling it flow against her fingers. The Crown Vic was parked haphazardly on the side of a dirt road. They had stopped somewhere near the Litchfield border. Neither was sure of what to do.

Finally, Adrian went to her. "Cole. We need to hurry."

She didn't respond. She pulled her hand from the river and watched the water drop from her fingertips.

"That woman," she whispered. "She took a clump of Lou's hair when he tried to arrest her. She snipped it off his head and then said something. She must have hexed him—turned him into a monster."

"I'm sorry about Lou, Cole." He knelt next to her. "I know you were close to him. But if we don't move now, then much worse things are going to happen to a lot more people. Do you understand? We have to get to the Gillespie house as soon as we can."

"I know." She took a stone from the dirt next to her boot, pitched it into the river, and then stood. "What is she doing with the people she's killing? Why the children? Why dig up Peter Bell?"

"She's using these victims deliberately. She has powers, Cole. You've seen them for yourself. We don't know the extent of them, but she can turn people into animals, breathe fire, and make decapitated heads talk."

"What if the people she's killing are some sort of sacrifice? For something involving her dead fiancé?"

"Like a resurrection ritual." Adrian paused. "She's using the children and the other victims to bring Peter back to life. It's the only thing that makes sense."

"We have to find her, Adrian. Once she has Peter back—"

"She's going to extract her revenge on the whole village."

They went to the Crown Vic and Cole popped the trunk. Amongst the flares, stop sticks, police tape and turnout gear, Cole pulled out a weapon case and took a shotgun with a box of shells from it. She loaded the shells into the gun and cocked the forestock to pump one into the chamber.

"Should we tell the Manchester police?" Adrian asked.

"I don't know. I've thought about it, but I don't think we should. They're in the dark about all of this. They haven't seen what we've seen. They don't know what this woman is capable of. It could be a mess. We need to move now. Get in the car."

The Gillespie property was barren. No lights were on inside the house, and the only sound was the light squeaks of a loose windshield frame in a hollowed-out truck sitting on cinder blocks blowing in the wind. There were no footprints in the snow leading to or from the front door. As far as Cole and Adrian could tell, the Gillespies had gotten no visitors.

They got out of the cruiser. "Stay behind me, Adrian," Cole said, gripping the shotgun and shutting the driver door with her boot.

The front door was unlocked. Cole turned the knob, and then used the barrel of the shotgun to push the door open. She fished an arm inside and slapped around until she hit the light switch. The living room lit up dimly. A recliner was knocked over and torn apart, with fabric and cotton strewn about the floor. The television was smashed, and blackening blood was smeared into the carpet. A draft was felt through the ripped-up screen door across the room. Bloody tracks went everywhere, up and down the hall, and all around the living room. It was difficult to see where they began or ended.

Cole stepped over the bloodstains. "It looks like our Canuck friend was here already."

Adrian knelt to examine the stains while Cole inspected the bathroom and bedroom. The bedroom was undisturbed, and it appeared that most of the carnage had occurred in the bathroom. The mirror, the sink and the toilet were all smashed, and the door was nearly ripped out of its frame. It was as if a wild animal had been locked inside and had fought its way out.

"You notice anything weird about these tracks, Cole?"

"Besides the fact that they're bloody and all over the fucking place? Not a thing."

"They look like animal tracks. Almost like hoof marks, with fingerprints around them.

The constable and Adrian gave each other a grave look.

The tracks ultimately seemed to lead out the back door. They were bright red in the fresh snow, crossing the backyard and venturing into the woods. Whatever had been in the house left not that long ago.

They stepped out and Cole took a flashlight from her belt and pointed it at the trees. "The tracks lead into the woods. If we're lucky, they'll lead us straight to Angelique."

It was pitch black within. The narrow cone of light cut through the dark like some hopeless lighthouse in a starless sea. Trees and the snow-patched ground was all that could be seen. The bloody prints were their only guidance.

Cole suddenly stopped and shot her arm out against Adrian's abdomen.

"What?"

"Listen."

Heavy breathing was heard, like a large exhausted animal.

"The fuck is that?" Adrian said.

Cole shined her light against a small grotto about a yard ahead. Something was moving around inside it. Two black eyes stared out at them from within.

Cole handed Adrian the flashlight, aimed the shotgun at the grotto, and then gestured her head at Adrian to keep behind her.

"Adrian, I need you to point your light this way, slightly down."

With some nervous hesitation, Adrian squatted and aimed the flashlight. A beast lay pathetic inside the grotto, staring at them like some sad pup. Its eyes were human, spaced between a large snout. The snout dripped snot and could be heard sniffling.

It had the naked body of a man, but the arms and legs were contorted and twisted, and the hands and feet were mutilated with what appeared to be sprouted hoofs.

The monster and Cole looked each other in the eyes for a long time. Cole recognized it to be Samuel Gillespie. Tears streamed from his eyes. It seemed to be pleading at her to kill it.

Once she had control over her stomach, she swallowed, aimed the shotgun and shot the pigman twice. The gunshots cracked throughout the forest. The pigman howled, snorted, and then went silent.

"It was Samuel," Cole said, her voice cracking. "We were too late."

"Where's his wife and daughter?"

"Angelique must have gotten to them. Samuel must have caught her and tried to intervene. She put a hex on him like she did with Lou, except instead of a bird she turned him into a pig."

"I don't know what we could have done to save him, Cole. You saw what happened to Lou. He must have been in agony."

"That doesn't make me feel better, Adrian."

"Angelique can't be far from here." Adrian began climbing over the grotto.

"Adrian, wait a minute."

"I have to find my niece, Cole."

"Adrian, you can't—"

"Don't!" he shouted. "There's still a chance. I have to see what Angelique is doing with her and the other children. Their mothers may be dead, but the children might still be alive."

Cole climbed up the grotto and caught up to him. She grabbed him by the back of the coat and yanked him back. "At least let me lead, you idiot! I'm the one with the gun. I've seen enough death this week, so I don't need you getting yourself killed."

"Look!" Adrian pointed.

Something glowed through the trees ahead. Cole raised the shotgun and moved forward, careful to avoid branches and dry leaves. A quiet humming could be heard, almost like a hymn.

"Adrian, shut off the flashlight."

He did so.

The ruins of the Bell house resembled an old crumbling cathedral. On the pillars, the brick foundations, and each step of the old staircase were hundreds of candles. Their light danced in the night beneath the blood moon, wavering against the trees.

In the center of the ruins was a concrete slab where skeletal remains were set. Kneeling around the slab with their arms reaching towards the moon were the three headless cadavers of Clarissa Holloway, Frances Gillespie, and Grace Davenport. Their heads circled above the slab, floating in the air, chanting in a language undecipherable.

Cole and Adrian watched the séance while hiding behind a waist-high stone wall.

"My God, Cole."

They watched, hypnotized by the scene as the decollated heads swam in the air over their worshipping bodies. Their voices cantillated in unison. The longer Cole and Adrian watched, the more they felt themselves becoming lightheaded; the séance influenced them in a way that couldn't be deciphered consciously. The light of the candles seemed to change color, radiating the ruins in stark contrasts of luminous oranges and reds, then purples and blues like St. Elmo's Fire.

All around the ruins, three tall wooden crosses had been erected, looking haphazardly put together. They were aligned in a triangle, all three facing the slab where the skeleton was laid out. Upon the crosses, the bloodied cadavers of Amy Gillespie, Jeremy Davenport and Julia Holloway hung.

At the sight of this, Adrian gasped and clapped his hand over his mouth. "No—dear God, no!"

"What? Keep your voice down, Adrian."

He pointed. "Look!"

Cole peeked over the wall and finally saw it. Immediately, she recoiled and turned her head away. The sight was horrific. She shut her eyes, but she still kept seeing what had happened to the children.

"Oh God, Julia," Adrian whimpered. He looked like he was ready to explode in a fit of emotion.

Cole opened her eyes, saw him, then reached out and grabbed him by the front of his shirt. "Adrian, you need to stay quiet. We cannot have them hear us."

"I'm sorry." Adrian clenched his teeth and wiped his face. He was struggling to regain his composure.

"We're going to get her, Adrian. Do you understand? We're going to kill her for this. Okay?"

"Okay."

They huddled against the wall and peeked over it again, both being very careful to not to look at the crosses, and what had become of the children.

Angelique stepped out from beneath the arch of the stone staircase, holding the skull of the skeleton in her hands. She approached the slab and held the skull up in the air to the red moon.

"It's Peter," Adrian whispered. "This is it."

All at once the heads stopped moving, and the chanting ceased. Angelique brought the skull down and turned to the stone wall. Cole and Adrian ducked. Neither said anything. They just squatted there, hoping that the witch hadn't seen them.

Something slithered towards them. The leaves shuffled, and something resembling a snake appeared. It snapped towards

Adrian, wrapped around his ankle and yanked him off the wall and towed him away.

"Adrian!" Cole stood.

Adrian was dragged away by a vine attached to a large tree near the wall, and it dangled him upside down several feet from the ground. He grabbed at the vine on his leg, unable to get it off.

"You're too late!" Angelique shouted. "I knew I had one more Holloway to take care of."

Cole pointed the shotgun at her. "Put him down now, Angelique!"

The veiled woman didn't remotely flinch at the sight of the firearm.

"I said put him down now!"

"Or what?"

Cole pulled the trigger. The recoil jerked her back, and she put a foot behind to keep herself from falling over. Angelique still stood. Cole racked the forestock and squeezed the trigger again, this time grasping the shotgun with all her strength to make sure that her shot didn't miss. The pillar behind the witch splintered, and chips of stone sputtered in a dusty haze. The shot went directly through her and did nothing to faze her.

The witch started to laugh.

Cole once more racked the forestock, then aimed the gun again and prepared to fire. Just as she pulled the trigger, Angelique raised her hand up to Cole and pointed. In that moment, the shotgun misfired, and Cole was thrown back onto the ground. The stench of melted metal and gunpowder stung her nostrils. She sat up, got into a kneeling position, aimed the gun again and pulled the trigger. The gun did not fire. She realized then that there was a huge rupture in the side of the barrel. Angelique had cast some sort of spell to make the gun jam when it was fired, and the shell and pellets imploded the barrel.

"Cole!"

Adrian hung, hopelessly trying to get the vine off him. The branches of the tree began to move and bend, like dozens of wooden arms. They grabbed Adrian by the arms and pulled on them. Several more branches began scraping and cutting him.

"Help me, Cole! Do something!"

The tree tore his clothes to shreds, sliced into his flesh and peeled large chunks out. The branches gripping his limbs pulled and pulled until one of his arms popped off. Warm blood splattered across Cole's face. The disembodied arm fell from the branch and landed against the cold soil next to her. Adrian screamed, and the branches began digging into his abdomen, ripping out his intestines.

"Vous mourrez tous," Angelique howled. She lifted her veil. Cole saw her ruined face, and her single eye was filled with fire. *"TOUS MEURENT!"*

The three heads flew towards Cole. Their rolled white eyes were bulging and their lips were peeled back, baring their bloodied teeth.

Cole didn't think. She dropped the ruined shotgun and ran, covering her face with her arms. The only thing she focused on was the ground, watching for patches of snow where the footprints she and Adrian had made earlier could lead her. The trees came alive as she fled, creaking and moaning as they shifted and reached for her. A branch clawed at her thigh and another tore a chunk of hair out of her scalp. The pain meant nothing. The instinct of self-preservation kept her moving.

Angelique laughed. The sound of it chased Cole through the woods. The gargling heads could be heard behind her as well, not more than a few feet away. Cole didn't dare look back. She just kept moving.

She made it into the backyard of the Gillespie house. Cole circled around the house and ran for the Crown Vic parked on the side of the road. She yanked open the driver door, threw herself in and slammed the door shut. Just as she jabbed her keys into the ignition, Clarissa Holloway's rotten head slammed into the windshield, cracking it. Its black tongue licked the glass and its teeth clinked against it.

Cole started the cruiser and stomped on the gas. The vehicle peeled down the street and Clarissa's head rolled off the windshield. Several times Cole nearly lost control of the car with the sharp turns that she was taking at the speed she was going. She didn't care. The only thing her body and mind told her to do was to get out of the village as fast as she could.

Eventually she saw the exit for I-93 and she pulled onto it. The blood from Clarissa's head was smeared all over the windshield, and in a flash of clarity Cole turned the knob for the windshield spray and ran the wipers.

The panic didn't falter until she neared the Massachusetts border. Her muscles relaxed, and she finally gained the courage to look in the rearview mirror. The heads were nowhere to be seen. Angelique's laughter was gone. She had escaped.

# November 5<sup>th</sup>

# Waning Gibbous

In the early hours of the morning, just as daylight was breaking, a young woman with dark, traumatized eyes stepped into a rest station motel just outside Providence, Rhode Island. She booked a room for a single night. She signed in under the name Jane Doe and every word that passed her lips sounded faint and unsteady. Judging by the uniform, she was some sort of cop, and by the look in her eyes, she had just survived something awful, so the receptionist didn't question her.

Cole spent the morning in her room standing by the window. Everything that she had seen replayed in her mind again and again. Bodies strewn on trees, floating heads, a man— someone she knew—getting ripped apart right before her eyes.

At noon, she sat on the end of her bed and turned on the TV. The news was reporting on a massive fire. A small township located in the city of Manchester, New Hampshire was burning to the ground. Fire departments from Manchester, Londonderry, New London and Sandown all converged on the village to try and put out the blaze.

According to eyewitnesses, the fire had begun rapidly and consumed everything it touched. There were no official estimates on the death toll, but it was "looking grim" according to an EMT. Where the fire had begun was a matter of speculation.

There was only one unusual shred of evidence that had emerged from the fiasco. From a gas station security camera near the interstate, an image was captured of a woman wearing a black dress and veil, holding hands and walking with an unidentified nude man. They passed by the camera's line of sight for mere seconds, and then they were gone. The police were making inquiries, but there was little means of identifying the two.

That night the moon transitioned to waning gibbous. The lunar cycle continued, with natural time passing between each phase thenceforth.

The ritual was over. Leinster Village became ashes.

*Ceremony of Ashes*

Thank you for purchasing *Ceremony of Ashes*.

If you enjoyed this book, please consider leaving a review on Amazon. Every review counts. If you'd like updates on future content, free promotions, giveaways, and more, then subscribe to my newsletter at www.jaysonrobertducharme.com.

J.R.D.

Printed in Great Britain
by Amazon

75965861R00085